CAHILLS vs. VESPERS

SHATTERPROOF

THE 39 CLUES

ROLAND SMITH

SCHOLASTIC INC.

NEW YORK TORONTO LONDON AUCKLAND
SYDNEY MEXICO CITY NEW DELHI HONG KONG

For the fearless foursome
Will, Jack, Ethan, and JR.
— R.S.

Library of Congress Control Number: 2012931144

ISBN 978-0-545-32413-7

10 9 8 7 6 5 4 3 2 1   12 13 14 15 16/0

Book illustrations by Charice Silverman for Scholastic
Photos of people: Ken Karp for Scholastic
Antikythera device pg. 83: AAAC/TopFoto/The Image Works
Rock texture for star pg. 175: CG textures

Library edition, September 2012

Printed in China 62

Scholastic US: 557 Broadway • New York, NY 10012
Scholastic Canada: 604 King Street West • Toronto, ON M5V 1E1
Scholastic New Zealand Limited: Private Bag 94407 • Greenmount, Manukau 2141
Scholastic UK Ltd.: Euston House • 24 Eversholt Street • London NW1 1DB

CHAPTER 1

On a bus to Berlin, Germany

"Bluetooth earpieces are so geeky," Dan Cahill said.

"But they free up your hands for surfing the web, stealing priceless jewels, and eating pastry," Atticus said, taking a huge bite out of an apple strudel.

"And picking your nose," Dan added, which caused Atticus to blow a mouthful of strudel all over the seat in front of them occupied by Dan's sister, Amy, who was trying to sleep.

Amy had heard the entire lame exchange — and felt the half-chewed pastry chunks splatter the back of her head — but she resisted the strong urge to turn around and tell the boys to shut up. She was happy that the old, goofy Dan was back, acting like a complete idiot. He had grown up way too much in the past few weeks, and she hadn't liked what he was turning into. Dan had seen too much, too fast, and lately she'd caught glimpses of something dark inside him.

And the pressure on the two of them was growing.

Vesper One was not just a step ahead, he was miles ahead of them. He not only knew what they were going to do before they did it, he even seemed to know what they were thinking. *But so far, no hostages have died*, she reminded herself. *We have handled every ridiculous and dangerous task Vesper One has thrown at us. Our friends are still alive.*

She wondered how much longer it could last.

Seven members of the Cahill family had been kidnapped and a man known only as Vesper One was threatening to kill them one at a time unless Amy and Dan delivered a series of bizarre ransoms. He was pulling their strings like a puppet master, teasing them, commanding them, and they had no choice but to obey. Which is why Amy found herself on a bus, in a snowstorm, moving doggedly toward their next target even though their flight had been canceled.

"I've discovered that Berlin is not the only place having weird weather," Atticus said to Dan.

Their long flight from Samarkand had barely landed in Heidelberg when the airport was closed due to the earliest snowfall in Germany's history. The airline company put the grumbling passengers on buses for a slushy six-hour drive to Berlin.

"There's a heat wave in Attleboro — upper nineties. In the Pacific Northwest, where some places get one hundred twenty–plus inches of rain, they're having a drought. Climatologists are scrambling to figure out the strange weather shift."

Dan wasn't paying attention. "You strudel-chunked your laptop!" he said.

This started another round of hysterical giggling, causing several other passengers to curse in German and "Shh!" them, which the boys completely ignored.

Amy shook her head in wonder. Listening to the two boys, you wouldn't know that a couple days earlier, Atticus had almost been murdered. She pulled a strudel chunk out of her hair. *It's as if none of it ever happened. But it did happen. Worse things have happened. . . .*

Amy looked out the window at the blowing snow in the gray waning light and pushed the worries firmly out of her mind. They were just entering Berlin, the site of their current assignment. Vesper One had sent them yet another cryptic ransom note on the satellite phone he had so kindly provided for them. Every time it chimed, Amy felt dread surge deep in her belly.

```
Well, time to celebrate. And what better
place than the cheerful city of Berlin?
Home of a priceless jewel, in a heavily
guarded museum. I trust you have heard
of it. Because your next assignment is
to liberate it. And deliver it to me.

Thanks in advance. And a jolly "Guten
Tag!" from Uncle Alistair.

Vesper One
```

The puppet master at work, Amy thought bitterly. *No mention of the name of the museum, which jewel, or how long we have to steal it before he murders one of our friends.*

Jake Rosenbloom, Atticus's older half brother, was sound asleep in the window seat next to her. He was an arrogant jerk, but she had to admit he was easy to look at, even with his brown eyes closed, his lips half open, and a tiny drop of drool leaking from the corner of his mouth. Looking at him, she found her lips fluttering upward into a smile until she caught herself and abruptly frowned.

There's nothing to smile about! she reminded herself.

The boys were uncharacteristically silent. Amy leaned out of her seat and looked back to see what trouble they had found. Dan had the window seat and was looking at his smartphone. Atticus was hunched over in the aisle seat, his dreads dangling over the laptop screen as his nimble fingers flew over the keyboard like a virtuoso pianist.

"Any luck figuring out which museum we're supposed to . . ." Amy didn't want to say "rob" for fear of being overheard.

Atticus shook his head. "There are over a hundred and seventy museums and galleries in Berlin. It's impossible to say which one of them has—"

"What we're looking for," Amy interrupted. Atticus was a genius, but he was only eleven years old. He sometimes forgot that anyone could be eavesdropping.

"Uh . . . right," he said, darting a quick look at their fellow passengers.

"We're here," Dan said, wiping the fog off the window with his hand. He looked at Amy. "What's your plan?"

"I don't have a plan, uh, Frederick."

"Frederick?" Dan said.

"Frederick Wimple," Amy said. It was just the latest of a series of fake identities, counterfeit passports, and forged birth certificates cooked up by a team of Cahills at their command center in Attleboro. *Where is Sinead coming up with these names?* Amy wondered.

"Just kidding," Dan said loudly, trying to cover his lapse. "You know I hate it when you call me Frederick. Call me Fred. If you don't, I'll start calling you Fi instead of Fiona."

"Sorry, Fred." Amy rolled her eyes.

The bus stopped and the interior lights came on.

Jake's eyes snapped open and he flinched in his chair. "Where are we?"

"Brandenburg International Airport," Amy answered.

Atticus stuck his head between the seats. "Berlin, bro. It's still snowing."

"Great," Jake said, wiping the corner of his mouth and working the kink out of his neck.

Amy smiled again, but when Jake caught the look and smiled back, she frowned and glared at him.

Dan narrowed his eyes. "What's with you, Fiona?"

"I'm just happy that we're getting off this bus," she snapped.

"Right," Dan said.

They found their rented Mercedes SUV deep inside the parking structure.

"I'll drive," Dan said.

"In your dreams, Frederick," Amy said. "You don't have a license."

"Shotgun!" Atticus said, jumping into the passenger seat.

"I didn't want to sit up there anyway," Dan claimed, climbing into the backseat next to Amy.

Jake settled into the driver's seat and started the engine, but before he could adjust his mirrors, flashing blue lights appeared behind them. A police car was blocking them in.

Amy's stomach lurched. *Interpol?* They were caught already. She met Jake's eyes in the rearview mirror.

"Maybe they're just checking out the rental cars leaving the parking lot," he suggested.

"And maybe they're not," Amy spat. "If we get arrested, a hostage will die!"

Two gigantic policemen got out of the car. "Exit the vehicle!" one of them shouted. *"Schnell!"*

"Remember, your name is Fred Wimple," Amy whispered to her brother as they climbed out of the SUV and lined up beside it.

"Passports!" the larger policeman snapped.

"They're in our bags," Jake said, keeping his voice calm and steady.

"Get them!"

"Sure. No problem. No need to shout." Jake popped the back hatch open, but as he reached in to grab his pack, the second policeman pushed him roughly aside.

"Hey!" Jake balled his hands into fists.

Amy signaled him with a small shake of her head. Something wasn't right about the two cops. *If they know, why don't they just arrest us? Why are they hassling us like this?*

Jake took a deep breath.

The second policeman pulled their things out onto the ground and turned to Amy. "Which one is yours?"

Amy pointed at a small blue backpack.

The policeman grabbed it, turned it upside down, and shook everything out.

Jake stepped forward, but Amy gripped his arm.

"Let it go," she whispered.

The policeman found Amy's fake passport, then rummaged through the other packs until he held all four in his hand.

"Your business in Berlin?"

"We're tourists," Amy stammered, her knees going weak.

"Name of your hotel?"

"We . . . we were just on our way to find one."

The policeman looked at Dan. "Frederick Wimple?"

"Right," Dan answered.

"Wrong," the policeman said. "Your passport is a forgery. Your name is Dan Cahill." He pulled his pistol from its holster. "And you are all under arrest!"

Amy let out a gasp of horror. Dan's head jerked toward the nearest exit. She followed his gaze. It was a hundred feet away. They'd never make it.

The second policeman pulled four sets of flex-cuffs off his belt. "Turn around and put your hands on your heads."

Jake stepped in front of the pistol, shielding the others.

"There's some kind of mistake," he said, trying to stall for time.

"No mistake. Turn around. All of you!"

There was an agonizing pause as they calculated their options and realized they didn't have any.

"We better do what he says," Amy said in defeat.

Reluctantly, Jake turned around with the others. Amy leaned against her brother, waiting for the plastic cuffs to squeeze around her wrists. Barely two steps into Berlin, and they'd already failed.

Which hostage will die? Which hostage have we just killed?

"Something's not right," Jake whispered.

"I'll say," Dan hissed back. "We're in a parking structure with two giants with badges, guns, and no witnesses. We need to get—"

Two doors slammed behind them, followed by

the screech of rubber on cement. Amy whipped her head around to see the police car barreling through the exit. For a second, the four kids were too stunned to move.

"Quick! Let's get out of here!" Amy said.

Just then, the Vesper phone chimed.

Ha-ha. Scared you! A bag within your bag. Replace the paste with the real one at the Pergamon Museum. Because of your late arrival you only have a couple hours before closing time. If you fail, it's Death-Oh-Clock for Uncle Alistair (per Dan's request), and perhaps I'll include the youngest as a special bonus . . . Cousin Phoenix. Oh, and speaking of dead things, I've wiped the phone you swiped from Luna. You can no longer get in touch with me. I'm very unhappy with you. I'll let you know what your punishment will be. Have a nice day. ☺

Vesper One

Dan slammed his fist into the car. "He's going to punish us through Alistair!"

Amy put a hand lightly on her brother's shoulder. "We don't know that."

"Amy's right," Jake said. "He's just messing with us.

The only way to keep our heads straight is to ignore him and stay on task."

Amy didn't like the look on Dan's face as he turned on Jake. "Easy for you to say. You don't even know Alistair!"

"Stop!" Amy ordered. "I've had enough testosterone in the past five minutes to last me a lifetime. We need to focus."

She picked up Luna's pink cell phone and tossed it to Dan. "Check the phone." She looked at Jake and Atticus. "Help me get this stuff back in my pack."

"Phone's toast," Dan said after a second. He threw it against a cement pillar and it burst into a hundred pink pieces.

"Was that necessary?" Amy asked.

"Probably not," Dan answered, "but it felt good."

Amy shook her head, then noticed something in the pile that hadn't been in her backpack earlier. It was a small black velvet bag. She picked it up.

"What's that?" Dan asked.

"'A bag within your bag,'" Atticus said.

Amy loosened the drawstrings and dumped a diamond the size of a marshmallow into her palm.

CHAPTER 2

Pompeii, Italy

> V-1: Contact established with the Cahills.
> Exactly where you'd expect. Will track.
> Can kill. Awaiting instructions.
> —V-4
>
> V-4: The trap is baited. V-5 is in place.
> Proceed.
> —V-1

Erasmus Yilmaz sat on the edge of a stone fullery in the city of Pompeii, wishing he didn't know that in ancient times, slaves used fulleries to wash their masters' clothes. In urine.

The fullery was indoors, but it gave him a good view of the square outside. Across from him was a large opening. He'd picked the spot so he could watch the crowds without being seen.

Pompeii is a dead city, he thought. *And coming here was a dead end. But where do we go next?*

Erasmus felt a rare grin cross his face.

We.

He hadn't thought in terms of a team since he was a boy.

On the run with Mom . . . The grin vanished.

When Erasmus was just three years old, his father was murdered by Vespers. Japan, Russia, India, Canada. Erasmus and his mom never spent more than a few months in any one location. Erasmus did not go to school, but he learned nine languages and read a thousand books during their run.

We.

They had almost started to believe the threat had faded when the Vespers finally struck. He was at his dojo when the fire broke out at their apartment complex. Several people had died, including Erasmus's mom. The Vespers were only too real.

Erasmus turned his attention back to the crowd on the square where at least a hundred people had gathered. A smoking Mount Vesuvius loomed above them, but no one was looking at the volcano. Their attention was focused on the *Disaster Watch!* television van and its famous meteorologist, Sandy "the Breeze" Bancroft.

Erasmus had no problem picking his partners out of the crowd. Hamilton Holt was a foot taller and wider than anyone else there. Jonah Wizard was wearing a black hoodie, even though it was a beautiful day. He had to be hot with the hood pulled over his famous head and the fake beard Erasmus was making him wear.

Erasmus hadn't been pleased when Amy teamed two teenagers up with him, but to his surprise he'd grown fond of them. They were both dedicated to the fight and willing to do anything — even travel with each other. The two boys were completely different. Erasmus grinned again. *Jonah has rap playing in his head, Hamilton wants to rap people on their heads.*

Erasmus had sent them into the crowd and told them not to speak to anyone. Their job was to mingle and listen. He knew that they wouldn't hear anything worthwhile, but that wasn't the point. He was training them, thinking that maybe one day, one of them would take his place.

He was about to call the boys in when a text came from Jonah.

```
Luna Amato is here.
```

`What's she doing?` Erasmus typed back, feeling a tide of anger well up in his chest.

```
Watching the weather dude.
```

`Did she recognize you?` Erasmus asked.

The response came immediately. Nope. And I'm standing five feet away.

What about Hamilton?

He's standing right next to me. He's hard to miss. She hasn't even looked at him.

Another text flashed across the screen. Wait! She's on the move.

Just five days before, William McIntyre, an important Cahill adviser and one of Erasmus's few friends, had been murdered in Rome. Luna was either in on the murder, or knew who did it. And Erasmus was determined to squeeze every bit of information out of her.

Follow her. Like I taught you.

Erasmus pulled a pair of binoculars out of his leather jacket and watched. Sure enough, it was Luna Amato. His jaw clenched as he zoomed in. The Vesper spy appeared harmless—she looked like a retired schoolteacher on a tour. But that's what made her so deadly. What allowed her to bring down people like William.

Erasmus lowered the binoculars and narrowed his eyes. All that was about to change.

He wasn't going to let the Vespers get away with murder again.

CHAPTER 3

Alistair Oh would have given anything for a bite of one of his steak burritos and a sip of something refreshing. Instead he was holding a cold baked potato and a paper cup with four ounces of murky water. The Vespers had shut off the hostages' water and reduced their food ration in retaliation for the recent escape attempt. Once a day, a sack with seven baked potatoes and a single quart of water was dropped down the shaft of the broken dumbwaiter.

"The Irish survived on a mostly potato diet for hundreds of years," Fiske Cahill pointed out, staring grimly at the spud in his hand.

"That's correct," Alistair agreed. "I did a great deal of research while working on my Frozen Peanut Butter–Potato Tot Burrito."

"How'd that sell?" Ted Starling asked. He was sitting near the damaged dumbwaiter, hoping to hear a snippet of conversation from their captors above.

"Not well, I'm afraid," Alistair said. "But I did learn that the average Irish citizen consumed five to eight pounds of potatoes a day, and they were healthy."

"We're getting about a pound a day for seven of us," Natalie Kabra pointed out. She prodded the shriveled spud on her plate, then stared in dismay at her hands. "Oh, my God! My hands look like monkey paws. I'd give anything for cream and an emery board."

"Your hands look fine," Ted said.

"No offense, Theodore," Natalie said. "But you're blind."

Alistair cut in before the kids could start squabbling. "A bigger concern is drinkable water," Alistair said. "We're getting dehydrated. We'll die of thirst long before we die of hunger."

"Let's try to think of the positive," Fiske said.

"Good idea," Natalie shot back. "Why don't you start, Fiske?"

"Well . . ." Fiske trailed off.

"Can it, Natalie," Nellie said. "If they get us fighting among ourselves we won't have the energy to fight them."

"In order to fight them, we have to get to them," Reagan said, out of breath from the crunches. She started doing one-handed push-ups with her good hand, but only managed six before losing her strength.

Phoenix waved Alistair over to where he and Nellie were sitting. "Is everything okay?" Alistair asked quietly.

Phoenix leaned over and whispered into his ear. "I think Reagan is going to die."

CHAPTER 4

As Jake drove the SUV through the dark, icy streets, Atticus's fingers flew across the laptop keyboard to try to identify the decoy diamond they'd been given.

"I've got it!" he shouted. "The diamond's called the Golden Jubilee. It's on loan from the king of Thailand, at the Pergamon Museum."

"Where is that?" Dan said, shifting in his seat.

"We're three blocks away," Jake said, pointing at the navigation screen.

They parked the SUV a block away from the Pergamon. They were on the scene, but they still didn't have the slightest idea how they were going to steal the diamond.

"It's one of the most heavily guarded museums in Berlin," Atticus said. He had the Pergamon website up on his laptop. "It's subdivided into the antiquity collection, the Middle East museum, and the museum of Islamic art. Chancellor Angela Merkel was there last week for the unveiling of the Golden Jubilee exhibit. The museum is visited by over a million people every year, making it the most popular—"

"We don't need an audio tour!" Dan snapped. "We need to just get in there and swap the diamonds."

Atticus flinched, but Dan didn't care. He reached for the door handle. "We only have two hours left!"

"Hold on," Amy said.

Dan gave her an exasperated sigh. "What?"

"We can't just waltz in there and expect to walk out with one of the most valuable treasures on earth," she said, panic creeping into her voice. "We need to figure out a plan."

"Fine. But make it quick." Dan looked pointedly at his watch.

"We'll each go in at ten-minute intervals," Amy said. "Interpol has probably sent our photographs to every museum in Europe. It'll be safer if we don't enter together." She pulled a red wig out of her pack.

"I'm not wearing that!" Dan said. When they flew to Samarkand, the Cahills in the Attleboro comm center had made him dress as a redheaded girl named Shirley Cliphorn.

"*I'm* going to wear it," Amy said, pulling it over her head and shooting her brother an irritated look.

"I'll wear a baseball cap," Dan said.

"Dan, you'll go in first and find out where the Golden Jubilee is. Atticus will go in next and try to figure out what kind of electronic surveillance and alarm security they have in the museum. I'll come in third with the fake diamond. We'll stay in touch on our Bluetooths and get together once we have the lay of the place."

"What about me?" Jake asked.

To Dan's disgust, his sister blushed before she answered. "Stay in the car, keep it running, and pick us up if we somehow pull this off."

"So I'm the driver," Jake said flatly.

Dan stared at his watch. "Minute's up. I'm outta here. See you inside."

He opened the door and stepped out into the cold evening, happy to be *doing* something rather than *talking* about doing something. It was still snowing big, sticky white flakes and there was at least two feet of accumulation on the sidewalk. He wouldn't be surprised to find the Pergamon had closed for the day while Amy jabbered their time away, as if Alistair or Phoenix wasn't about to be murdered.

If it's closed, how do we get the diamond?

He reached the huge entry square to the museum and his shoulders instantly relaxed. People were still walking through the front doors into the building. A bus pulled up to the curb behind him, and a group of students close to his age filed out. None of them were wearing baseball caps, so Dan took his off and joined them as they hurried across the square. A couple of the kids said something to him in German, which he didn't understand. He smiled and nodded, hoping they weren't asking him if he was the notorious art thief Dan Cahill, aka Fred Wimple, aka Shirley Cliphorn.

Apparently they were just being friendly, because they smiled back and lined up behind their teachers.

Dan inserted himself into the group and walked inside with them. Every security checkpoint had Berliners shaking snow off their coats, hats, and umbrellas as they shuffled through. He tapped his Bluetooth.

"It's packed," he whispered.

"What's security like?" Amy asked.

"Tough." Dan put his pack on the conveyor belt. "X-ray machines and metal detectors. On the bright side, they don't seem to be paying much attention to what people look like. They didn't give me a second glance. Is Atticus on his way?"

"He just got out of the car."

"See you later."

"Dan?" Amy hated it when Dan hung up on her.

Jake turned and looked at her from the front seat. "Well?"

"Dan's inside," she said, keeping her frustration with her little brother to herself.

"Get into the front seat with me," he ordered.

Amy frowned at him. "Why?"

"Because it looks suspicious that you're in the back-seat and I'm in the front seat," Jake said impatiently.

Amy got out of the back, not because he wanted her to, but because he was probably right . . . again.

She didn't know what to think about Jake. Seventy-five percent of the time he was a jerk. The other twenty-five percent of the time he was asleep.

She got into the front seat and closed the door. She could feel the heat from his body and smelled something spicy mingling with the leather of the seats—it was annoyingly pleasant.

"What's the problem?" he asked. "What's bothering you?"

"Aside from being wanted by Interpol, trying to save seven hostages, and steal a priceless diamond?"

Jake smiled at her. "Yeah, aside from that."

Amy gave him a searching look, and then decided to answer honestly. "Dan," she said. "I'm worried about him. It's not right that a thirteen-year-old knows as much as he does about stealing things."

"You're right," Jake said. "He should have been at least sixteen like you before he became part of an international crime ring." He paused. "But I hear you. Atticus already knows more than I will in my entire life. It's scary. On the one hand he's a little kid, on the other hand he's a supercomputer with two legs. And then there's this whole Guardian thing."

On her deathbed, Atticus's mother, Astrid, Jake's stepmother, had told Atticus that she was a Guardian and that she was passing the responsibility on to him. But what that meant and how to do it was anyone's guess.

"What do you know about them?" Jake asked.

"Guardians?"

Jake nodded.

"Not much," Amy answered, not quite meeting his eyes.

This was more *truthish* than true. What she wasn't telling Jake was that she suspected one of the things the Guardians were protecting was a Cahill family relic, a gold ring currently hidden in plain sight on her wrist around the face of her Swiss watch. Only a handful of people knew about the ring's existence. The Vespers wanted it—badly enough that they'd nearly killed Amy trying to get it.

Time to change the subject. She looked at her watch. "Atticus should be inside the Pergamon by now."

"I'm going into the museum with you."

"No."

"I'm Atticus's *brother*. He's my responsibility."

"The best way you can keep him safe is to stay here and keep the car running." Jake opened his mouth to reply, but Amy jumped out of the SUV before he could argue further.

That's one way to handle him, she thought with a grin. Then she realized she was smiling. Again.

CHAPTER 5

Atticus was not thinking about keeping safe. He was standing in the security line thinking about being an international diamond thief.

Hanging out with Dan is so cool!

To pull the heist off, he would have to find the switch. All buildings had one. *Well, not mud-and-dung huts, but if there's electricity, there's a switch*, Atticus reasoned. Without power there were no lights, and more importantly no surveillance cameras, pressure plates, or alarms. He hoped Dan and Amy had flashlights in their packs, or a flashlight app on their smartphones.

He emptied his pockets and put his pack on the conveyor belt. As he walked through the metal detector, he asked the guard if he could talk to the person in charge of security.

"That would be Herr Rommel," the guard answered in German. "The man in the black suit." He pointed at the circular security counter in the center of the ornate lobby.

Atticus nodded. He recognized Rommel from a photo he'd seen on the Pergamon web page. He gathered his things, and his courage, and walked over to the security counter. Rommel was impeccably groomed, from his styled white hair to his perfectly manicured fingernails, creased slacks, and polished black shoes. He was going through a stack of papers as Atticus approached.

"*Guten Abend*, Herr Rommel," Atticus said in nearly flawless German.

Rommel looked up from his papers with piercing gray eyes. "*Guten Abend*. How may I help you?"

"My name is Atticus Rosenbloom, and I'd like a behind-the-scenes tour of the museum."

Rommel gave a short laugh. "I am not a tour guide. I am the director of security."

Atticus smiled. "Yes, I know. And that's why I decided to ask you. I'm doing a school assignment on museum security. In actuality, I'm not interested in how artwork and national treasures are displayed. I want to know how they are protected."

"And what school do you go to?"

"Harvard," Atticus lied. Technically, he'd only taken a few extension classes there, but Rommel didn't need to know that.

Rommel put the papers down and his gray eyes narrowed. "Really?"

"Yes." Atticus flashed his student identification card.

Rommel looked at it. "And you are how old?"

"Eleven. My father is Dr. Mark Rosenbloom, the archaeologist. I believe that you have some of his artifacts in your collection." Atticus didn't know if this was true or not, but it wouldn't surprise him. His father's discoveries were displayed in museums all over the world.

"I don't know your father's name, or his artifacts," Rommel said. "I am not a curator. I am only interested in security." He gave Atticus a thorough once-over. "You are a child prodigy?"

"I guess." Atticus didn't like the term. It made him sound like some kind of sideshow freak. Atticus glanced at his watch. Time was running out. Amy would be walking in soon and he'd learned absolutely nothing about the Pergamon's security system. "What about the tour?"

Rommel shook his head. "I am afraid I cannot accommodate you. I do not give tours, and we will be closing soon."

"That's disappointing," Atticus said with a crushed look. "Frau Bundeskanzlerin told me that you gave her a fabulous tour last week."

A look of astonishment crossed Rommel's face. "Are you referring to Chancellor Merkel?"

"Yes. She's an old family friend. I'm staying at her residence . . . well, until tomorrow, anyway. I fly back to the States in the morning. Anyway, I told her about my paper and she said that she was here last week and that you had been very kind and—"

"I only spoke to Chancellor Merkel for a moment," Rommel interrupted, smiling with delight. "I'm surprised she remembered me."

Atticus would not have known Chancellor Merkel if she walked up and kissed him. He'd only read about her visit to the Pergamon on the Internet twenty minutes earlier in the front seat of the car.

"You must have made a very positive impression," Atticus said, turning to leave. "I'll say hello to her for you."

"Wait, wait!" Rommel hurried out from the security station.

Gotcha! Atticus thought. It was all he could do not to pump his fist. He wiped the glee off his face, turned around, and nearly fainted. The top sheet of the papers Rommel was holding was clearly visible. It was an Interpol wanted poster.

On it was a photograph of Dan and Amy.

Rommel smiled. "Don't look so disappointed. I will give you a tour. A friend of Chancellor Merkel's is a friend of mine."

"Thank you," Atticus managed, though his mouth had gone as dry as parchment.

"Let me drop these off at the security line and we will begin."

As Rommel walked over to the line, Atticus hit Amy's speed-dial number with a trembling finger. She answered on the first ring.

"Where are you?" Atticus asked.

"I just got inside. I'm standing near the entrance. Who's the guy you were talking to?"

"Mr. Rommel. Head of security. You see those papers he just handed to that guard?" Atticus replied.

"Yeah."

"The top one is a wanted poster for you and Dan!"

Dan had not gotten very far into the Pergamon before he hit a one-hundred-by-forty-seven-foot wall: the Ishtar Gate. He was not much of a museum guy, and the gate had nothing to do with the Jubilee Diamond, but it was impressive enough to stop him in his tracks. He quickly glanced at the information tag.

The Ishtar Gate, he read, was one of the eight gates of Babylon, built around 600 B.C. by King Nebuchadnezzar and dedicated to the goddess Ishtar. It was discovered by a German archaeologist named Robert Koldewey in 1899, moved to Berlin piece by blue-tiled piece, and reconstructed inside the Pergamon. The bright tiles were lined with alternating rows of golden aurochs, which Dan learned were a type of extinct wild oxen, and dragons. But what really caught his attention was the compass etched beneath one of the aurochs. Dan leaned over the velvet rope for a closer look.

His breath caught in his throat. *This can't be a coincidence!*

It was the same symbol they had found on the de Virga map.

CHAPTER 6

Atticus was in the Pergamon's state-of-the-art security room, staring nervously at a bank of high-definition video monitors.

"A single door serves as both the entrance and the exit to the Golden Jubilee room. Everyone is counted going in and out," Rommel explained, pointing to the screen.

He pointed to another monitor, which showed the huge diamond from three different angles. Two grim-faced armed guards sandwiched the case. "The case is bulletproof," he said. "And bombproof, and fireproof, as is the room in which the Jubilee is kept. That was just one of the many conditions the king of Thailand had before loaning the jewel to the Pergamon. The museum has no surveillance dead areas."

The video array was impressive, but Atticus knew that Rommel was not being completely truthful. It was illegal to put video cameras inside restrooms.

"We are using the same technology as your Las Vegas casinos," Rommel continued with pride. "We even have facial recognition software."

Uh-oh.

"How's that work?" Atticus asked innocently.

"Step over here and I will demonstrate."

Rommel sat Atticus down at a computer terminal behind the monitors, then leaned over him to type in a string of numbers. Atticus followed his fingers intently, trying to memorize the access code.

"Here we go." Rommel clicked an icon.

Several video feeds from the Golden Jubilee room came onto the monitor. Atticus scanned the frames and tried not to scream when he saw Dan standing in line to get into the room.

Rommel moved the arrow of the cursor toward Dan's head.

"Can I do it?" Atticus asked, almost grabbing the cursor out of Rommel's hand.

"Certainly. Just click on someone in line."

Atticus moved the cursor as far away from Dan as he could get. He clicked on a woman at the end of the line, with two children who looked bored out of their minds.

"It is unlikely she is going to come up in our database," Rommel said. "In fact, it is unlikely any of the patrons in line, or in the room, will result in a hit. We only use the software when we identify someone acting suspicious. And we usually identify them while they are going through security."

"What if they wear a disguise?" Atticus asked.

Rommel gave a thin smile. "You can lose weight, gain weight, change your hairstyle, hair color, eye color, but you cannot change your bone structure. The software sees through all of these disguises."

Atticus thought about texting Amy and telling her not to act suspicious but then squirmed. If someone told him not to act suspicious, he'd immediately look twice as guilty as before.

"So if you're wanted by the police, your face is in the software database?" Atticus asked.

"Not just *wanted*." Rommel took over the cursor. Atticus held his breath, then let it out when Rommel switched to the video feed near the Ishtar Gate. He zoomed in on a middle-aged man. "Notice how he is not paying attention to the wall like the other patrons."

Atticus nodded. The man was looking everywhere but at the art.

"He was acting the same way as he went through the security line," Rommel continued. "Very suspicious. Go ahead and click on him."

Atticus clicked the mouse. A symbol appeared in the upper right-hand corner of the screen followed by the man's name.

INSPECTOR
MILOS VANEK_
INTERPOL
AGENT_

Atticus tried not to faint.

"So you can see that our facial recognition software not only identifies criminals," Rommel explained, "but it also identifies those who are pursuing criminals. Interpol stands for International Criminal Police Organization. We don't know who Agent Vanek is looking for, or even if he is after someone. We just know that he's in the building. We do not ask him what he is doing here. We just simply keep an eye on him. If he needs assistance, of course we will be happy to help."

Atticus knew exactly who Agent Milos Vanek was looking for. Vanek was the Interpol agent who had been hunting Amy and Dan Cahill since they committed their first crime for Vesper One. But how did Vanek know Amy and Dan were here? Atticus had to warn them, but Rommel was standing right over him.

"Why don't we switch places?" Atticus suggested, taking his smartphone out. "I need to get some of this down for my report. You can demonstrate while I take notes."

"Very good." They switched places. "I'll demonstrate how we can track . . ."

Atticus tuned Rommel out as he typed the bad news to Amy.

Dan was surprised to see there was only one door in and out of the Golden Jubilee room. People entered on the right side and exited on the left. An alert guard stood in the middle of the entrance, directing traffic and staring at everyone with steely blue eyes. Dan smiled at him as he passed. The guard did not smile back.

The glittering Jubilee Diamond was cordoned off by red velvet ropes. A mass of people circled their way past for a quick look, then moved on to the lesser jewels in the exhibit farther along the ropes. There were four armed guards standing in the middle of the rope circle, each facing a different direction. Above them were at least a dozen security cameras that swiveled constantly up and down, and back and forth.

Dan silently cursed Vesper One. Stealing the Jubilee was impossible.

Alistair Oh was going to die.

Amy stood in the security line, her backpack on the conveyor belt, her pockets empty except for the fake Jubilee Diamond, and her nerves completely frazzled.

Just before she stepped into line, they shut down two of the three security stations and announced that the museum would be closing in half an hour. This caused a bottleneck in the remaining line, and it was moving with agonizing slowness.

Amy's phone buzzed. She pulled it out and saw that she had a text from Atticus. She opened it and froze in place.

```
Milos Vanek is in the building.
```

The person in line behind her bumped into her back, and Amy let out a small scream.

"Sorry," she apologized, her face full of heat. She shuffled forward, scanning the room for Agent Vanek, wondering if the people around her could hear her heart pounding in her chest. She began to write a text to Dan, but didn't get very far.

"You will have to put the phone on the belt, Fraülein," a guard said, handing her a tray.

"Oh—oh . . ." she stammered. "Of course. Sorry."

Get ahold of yourself! Breathe.

She put her cell on the belt and tried to give the guard a smile, then remembered her watch and slipped it into a separate tray.

"Nothing metal in your pockets?"

Amy shook her head.

The guard nodded and Amy stepped through the detector. Alarms began to blare and red light blazed out across the room. To her horror, Amy became the instant focus of every pair of eyes in the room.

"We have one," a woman scanning the monitors said.

Rommel and Atticus turned around from the computer, and bile crept up Atticus's throat. Amy was on the big screen, surrounded by three guards.

"She was acting a little suspicious in line," the woman said. "But I didn't think anything of it until the detector sounded."

Rommel got up from the chair. "It's probably nothing, but let's run the facial program on her for our guest."

"You-you don't have to do that for me," Atticus stammered. "I'm actually a lot more interested in how you can follow people from one end of the museum to the —"

"This will only take a minute," Rommel interrupted. "And it's just a teenager, so we probably won't get a hit. Zoom in on her. Run the program."

Rommel's eyes widened, and then his lips curved into a hunter's smile. "As you might say in America, bingo!"

Atticus stared at the screen in defeat. Amy was standing with her arms out to the side. In the upper right-hand corner of the monitor was an alert.

"Locate Agent Vanek!" Rommel said.

A video of Milos Vanek appeared on one of the smaller screens. He was standing inside the Jubilee room, but he was not looking at the diamond.

"What's he staring at?" Rommel asked.

The guard started to flip through the cameras in the room.

Atticus already knew who Vanek was trailing. He quietly backed away from Rommel and the others to the computer terminal they had been using. He typed in Rommel's password and found the menu he was looking for.

Time to flip the switch.

The lights went out, then came back on a second later as the backup generator kicked in.

There's more than one switch!

Atticus killed the generator with five keystrokes, but the lights came on once again as the batteries took over.

Rommel turned around and glared at him.

"What are you doing?" he shouted, striding toward Atticus.

Atticus continued typing. He had to change the password before he hit the last switch or they would have the system back up in seconds.

"Step away from that keyboard!" Rommel lunged for him.

As Atticus dodged the enraged security chief, he managed to flip the final switch. The security room and the museum were plunged into complete darkness. Rommel started bellowing out orders. "Code red! Secure the rooms! We need lights! Find the boy!"

Atticus crawled as far away from the shouts as he could. He had positioned himself so he was facing the security door, but now in the pitch-black he wasn't sure if he was moving in the right direction. A flashlight flicked on, then another. The beams started to comb the room.

"I can't reboot the system!" someone shouted. "The passcode doesn't work!"

"The boy!" Rommel said. "Find him!"

Atticus started hyperventilating. His heart was slamming in his chest. They would be on him any second.

A flashlight beam swept along the far wall.

The door!

He crawled as fast as he could.

CHAPTER 8

Dan was crawling, too.

The sudden blackout caused pandemonium in the Jubilee room. People screamed and rushed the exit as the dark enveloped them. Dan was knocked to the floor. As he got to his hands and knees he was smacked down again. Someone stepped on his face. Another person clomped over his back. He was terrified, but not because of the dark, or the stampede. A second before the lights went out, he had seen the triumphant face of Milos Vanek staring right at him.

Dan crawled over to a wall and curled into a fetal position to make his body the smallest possible target. Every time someone kicked or bumped against him, he wondered if it was Milos Vanek catching up with him at long last.

The guards shouted for everyone to relax and stay where they were, but their commands were drowned out by the general hysteria.

Dan took a deep breath and tried to calm himself down. *Think! This isn't over yet. I'm ten feet away from the diamond in a pitch-black room.* He watched the guards' flashlight beams, trying to gauge where they were and what they were doing. What he saw was not good. All of the beams were concentrated around the Jubilee case. There was a sweep of light and Dan saw the guards illuminated. They had their guns drawn.

His heart sank. *Even if I got past them, I'd still have to get the case open.*

His Bluetooth pinged. "Dan?" It was Amy. She sounded out of breath.

"What?"

"Milos Vanek is in the museum!"

"I know. He's in the room with me somewhere," Dan said, his eyes still fixed on the cluster of guards around the diamond. "Where are you?"

"I'm with Atticus. He managed to slip out of security after switching off the lights. Rommel and the guards are looking for us. The police just arrived to secure the building. Atticus says the lights could come back on at any minute."

"Then get out," Dan said.

"What about the diamond? What about you?"

"I've got a plan. See you at the car." Dan pocketed the phone and looked at the silhouettes of the guards surrounding the case.

What's the worst that could happen? he thought as he crawled toward the Jubilee.

An unseen hand reached out from the darkness and grabbed Dan's arm in a viselike grip. Dan tore himself away and jumped to his feet. The guards pointed their flashlights at the commotion and he caught a glimpse of his assailant.

It was Vanek.

The agent lunged for him. Dan dodged away and slammed into one of the jewel cases. Vanek tripped and fell.

"Interpol!" Vanek shouted. "Arrest him!"

Dan expected the guards to shoot him, or at least gang-tackle him, but they stayed exactly where they were, protecting the Golden Jubilee. He ducked under their flashlight beams and tried to feel his way out of the black room.

If I'm arrested, it's game over. The Jubilee will have to wait.

He glanced back over at the guards. The shadow of a man was standing in front of them, shouting in German. He couldn't understand what he was saying, but it had to be Vanek demanding their help. The guards didn't budge from their positions, but Dan could see a flashlight beam bounce around the room, searching. Vanek had borrowed a light.

Dan stood and took off for where he hoped the exit was.

"Stop!"

He pressed through the panicked crowd trying to get through the door.

"Interpol! Stop him!"

Vanek's shouts echoed closer and closer behind him

as he clawed his way past screaming tourists. Interpol's finest was only inches away.

"Do we wait for Dan?" Atticus asked, breathing hard.

"We leave together or we don't leave at all," Amy said as she frantically scanned the people stumbling through the darkness.

People were using the light of their cell phones to find the exit. Some of them were injured and being helped by others.

"The lights are thinning out," she said. "It'll be hard for us to hide without a crowd."

"Try calling him again," Atticus suggested.

Amy hit his speed dial. It rang and rang, then went to voice mail. . . .

"Dan here. The reason I didn't pick up is because I'm probably eating something delicious. Leave a message and I'll—"

Someone wrapped their arms around Amy from behind. She screamed and jerked her head toward Atticus. A second man had grabbed him at the exact same moment. *Rommel!* She tried to stomp on her captor's foot, but he danced away and threw her to the ground. Her arms were wrenched behind her back and she felt the cold bite of handcuffs snapping around her wrists.

"Sorry . . . sorry . . . excuse me . . . sorry . . . *umph* . . . sorry . . ."

Dan stopped near the Ishtar Gate to catch his breath. He hadn't seen Vanek's flashlight beam in a couple of minutes, but he knew the Interpol agent was somewhere behind him in the dark. He wondered if he should double back and take another shot at the diamond now, or find a place to hide and tackle it later, after the museum emptied out. He looked at his watch and nearly vomited. There would be no later. Their time was up.

Someone is going to die.

The litany pounded across his brain until he couldn't focus on anything else. The horror of it burst out of his mouth in a terrible scream, and he didn't care if everyone in Berlin heard him. That's when his legs were pulled out from under him. He hit the marble floor hard and all the air rushed out of his lungs. As he lay gasping for breath, a flashlight clicked on, illuminating the jack-o'-lantern face of Agent Milos Vanek. Dan tried to get away, but found himself cuffed to Vanek's wrist.

"I go where you go," Vanek said. "We will wait here until the lights come back on. Perhaps we can have a nice conversation while we watch the people bump into each other." He scooted under the velvet rope near a stanchion and leaned against the wall of the Ishtar Gate.

Dan had no choice but to join him.

"Why were you screaming?"

Dan didn't answer. At the moment he was almost angrier at himself than he was at Vesper One. How could he have let Vanek sneak up on him?

"Cat has tongue? Okay. Change subject. I assume your sister is in the museum."

"If you don't let me go, someone is going to die," Dan said, surprised to feel hot tears of frustration running down his face.

"No need for tears. I can help. I am a policeman."

"I'm not crying," Dan said, turning his face away. "And I don't need your help. I just need you to let me go."

"That might be possible," Vanek said. "After you tell us about stealing the Caravaggio 'Medusa' and the Marco Polo manuscript, and your escape from jail. When I get you and your sister into headquarters I should not take more than a week to straighten this out."

Dan did not have a week, or a day, or a minute. He dragged a hand across his face to wipe the tears away. He didn't have time for crying, either. Vesper One could kill all of the hostages in a week.

"The Caravaggio painting we took from the Uffizi Gallery was a fake," he said. "We found the real one and it was returned. No one even knew the Marco Polo manuscript existed, so you can't very well accuse us of stealing it. As for the jailbreak, we didn't escape. Your coworker Luna Amato let us out."

"Luna Amato is not my coworker!" Vanek spit the words out like he had just taken a bite of cow dung. Dan felt spittle spray his face. "She is a traitor! If I could just get my hands on her I would . . ." Vanek raised his hands like he was throttling someone. "Wait a minute, what!?"

Dan stood up, rubbing his wrist. "Sorry, Milos, I gotta go." He reached down and took the flashlight and grabbed his pack.

Lightfinger Larry would have been proud. While Vanek was talking, Dan had lifted his keys and wallet. He had removed the handcuff from his wrist and reattached it to a stanchion.

"Unlock these cuffs!" Vanek shouted.

Dan raced off, taking little satisfaction in getting away from the Interpol agent. He ran across the lobby, trying to keep back fresh tears, his thoughts focused on the diamond. His only hope was that Amy had found a way to grab it. People were pouring out through the front doors. The police and television crews had arrived and were setting up equipment. He was reaching for his cell to call Amy when someone grabbed him. But Dan wasn't going to be taken again. He swung the heavy flashlight.

"It's me!" a familiar voice shouted as Jake wrenched the flashlight out of his hand.

"I thought you were in the car," Dan answered lamely.

"I got tired of waiting. And it's lucky I did. I got

here just in time to see two guys manhandle Atticus and Amy through there." He pointed the flashlight at a door.

Museumswache

BETRETEN VERBOTEN

"'Security. Do not enter,'" Jake translated.

"We have to get Atticus and Amy out of there."

Jake nodded. "Where were you?"

"Up in the Jubilee room with Milos Vanek."

"He's here?"

Dan explained what had happened.

Jake's voice brightened. "So you have his wallet?"

Dan took it out. "And his car keys."

"We don't need the keys for what I have in mind." Jake raised his eyebrow. "Do you *really* know how to drive?"

Despite the tears and the tight feeling in his chest, Dan managed a weak smile as Jake explained what he wanted to do.

This sounded like Dan's kind of plan.

CHAPTER 9

Amy and Atticus had been handcuffed together and pushed into two hard chairs against the wall. Rommel stood in front of them, flicking a flashlight beam on their faces as he interrogated them. So far neither one had answered any of his questions, which seemed to make him very angry. A guard stood nearby, shifting from foot to foot, and Amy could only guess that he was a little uneasy watching his boss yell at two children. Amy was trying to think of a way of taking advantage of the guard's nerves when there was a knock at the door.

"Tell whoever it is to go away," Rommel shouted.

The guard opened the door, spoke to the visitor for a moment, then walked back and whispered something to Rommel.

"Really?" Rommel said. "By all means, let him in. Perhaps these two will talk to Interpol."

Atticus leaned over to Amy and whispered, "Milos Vanek?"

"It must be," Amy whispered back.

"What do you —"

"No talking!" Rommel shouted, then turned to the man walking into the security room. "Agent Vanek. We are honored to have you here."

"I am not Agent Vanek," the man said. "I am Gale Monist." He flashed an Interpol badge. "Vanek and I are working together. I'm looking for him."

Amy and Atticus tried to hide their surprise. They knew that voice. The flashlight showed a man wearing a trench coat and hat, who looked like he had a mustache, although it was hard to tell in the dark.

"Agent Vanek was in the museum just before we lost power," Rommel said. "I couldn't tell you if he is still in the building or not. Have you tried his mobile?"

"Of course," Agent Monist said impatiently. "He's not answering, which is why I knocked on your door. And you are . . . ?"

"Alberich Rommel, Director of Security."

Agent Monist turned toward them. "And these are . . . ? My God! Amy Cahill! She's the reason Vanek and I are here. Who's the boy?"

"Her accomplice, I believe, but both of them refuse to answer my questions."

"We'll see if a trip to Interpol loosens their tongues," Agent Monist said.

"Not before they answer *my* questions," Rommel said. "Until they do, they will remain in my custody."

"Your custody?" Agent Monist's voice rose. "I wasn't aware that the Pergamon had a sanctioned police organization."

"Of course it doesn't," Rommel said. "But I apprehended them here and before they leave I must determine what damage they have caused to our collection."

"I see," Agent Monist said. "How did you lose your power?"

"The boy."

Agent Monist stared at Atticus. Atticus looked away, trying not to smile.

"I assume your power grid is controlled in this room."

"Yes."

"How did the boy get inside?"

Rommel hesitated. "I was giving him a tour."

"So, you *let* him in?"

Before Rommel could answer, Agent Monist got a call. He took his cell phone out of his trench coat.

"Yes . . . Where are you? . . . I'm inside the museum. . . . They have Amy Cahill and a boy. . . . No. A Herr Rommel wants to talk to them first. . . . I see. . . . Just stay where you are and I'll be out in a minute." He put the phone back in his pocket and looked at Rommel. "That was Milos Vanek. He's waiting out front for me in the car. He said that the news organizations have shown up. I suspect they will be wanting to talk to you about how this all happened. How you let the boy in the security room, how your security was breached by children, et cetera, or I can . . . Oh, never mind." He turned to leave.

"Wait," Rommel said. "Or you can what?"

Agent Monist turned back. "Or, I can take them out of here very, very quietly and when you speak to the media you can say that you don't know how the power went off, but Interpol is investigating. If they call us, which they will, we will back you up without giving them any details about your . . ." He paused. "Your unfortunate *tour*." He looked at his watch. "I have to leave. Agent Vanek and I are due back at headquarters for an important meeting."

"Take them," Rommel said with disgust. "And if you can get the boy to tell you the passcode he used to lock our system, it would be greatly appreciated."

"We'll get the passcode out of him," Agent Monist said. "And everything else he knows. You two come with me."

Amy and Atticus jumped to their feet.

Rommel escorted them to the entrance of the museum, but quickly faded back as soon as he saw the news vans outside.

Agent Monist, aka Jake Rosenbloom, draped his trench coat over the handcuffs so the news people wouldn't notice them as they hurried across the square.

"Where's Dan?" Amy asked.

"Agent Vanek is in the car, waiting for us at the curb."

Amy and Atticus climbed into the back of the SUV. Jake went around to the driver's side and opened the door.

"Scoot over."

"I got it," Dan said, his hands on the steering wheel.

"Forget it, Dan," Amy said.

"I drove it here."

"One block," Amy said. "Move over. There are police everywhere. We have to get out of here."

"Without the diamond," Dan said. His face was ashen.

"We'll talk about it as we drive."

Dan scooted over. Jake pulled away from the curb and left the Pergamon disaster behind.

CHAPTER 10

Jake drove the Benz several blocks north, then pulled into a parking lot.

"What are you doing?" Amy asked.

It was the first words any of them had spoken since leaving the museum. In a few minutes, the Vesper phone would *ping* with the news that one of their friends had died.

"This mustache is driving me crazy," Jake said. "I need to get it off me."

Dan got out of the front seat and opened the back door. He unlocked Amy's and Atticus's handcuffs with Agent Vanek's key.

"I'll sit back here with Atticus," he said.

Amy got into the front seat with Jake.

"How did Vanek figure out you were in the Pergamon?" Jake asked, pulling back into traffic.

"I didn't get a chance to discuss it with him," Dan answered flatly.

"Maybe he's a Vesper," Atticus suggested.

"Not likely," Dan said. "You should have heard

him when I mentioned Luna Amato, who we *know* is a Vesper. If she had been there, he would have strangled her."

"It's a good question," Amy said. "How did he know? He was inside the museum before we got there."

"All I know is that it'll be a while before he picks up our trail again," Dan said. "I have his passport, cash, credit card, and keys, thanks to Lightfinger Larry."

"Who?" Atticus asked.

"I'll tell you about him later," Dan said. "What I want to know is what set off the metal detector."

Amy shook her head. "I don't know. All I had in my pocket was the diamond. I'd even taken off my belt and my—"

She stopped in midsentence and started frantically going through her backpack.

"What?" Jake said.

"What are you looking for?" Dan asked.

"My watch!"

Dan's stomach lurched. "Are you sure?"

Amy threw the last of her gear out of the pack and held it upside down. "It's not here. We need to go back to the Pergamon."

"Are you kidding?" Atticus said. "The place is crawling with police. They know who we are."

"We'll get you another watch," Jake said.

"Not like the one she had," Dan said. He and his sister exchanged a panicked look. "Are you sure you left it there?"

"As soon as the lights went out, I grabbed my pack and the tray with my cell phone, but I completely forgot about the tray with the watch. How could I be so stupid?"

"Don't beat yourself up," Jake said. "Tomorrow, when things settle down at the museum, I'll go to their lost and found and pick up your watch. I bet there were plenty of things left there when the lights went out."

"That won't work!" Amy yelled. "I'm an idiot!" She pounded her fists on the dashboard as hard as she could. Tears streamed down her face.

For a second, everyone froze. Dan glanced at Atticus and saw that his eyes were as wide as Dan's were. Amy did *not* freak out like this. But she was slamming her fists down over and over again until Jake reached over and grabbed her, pinning her arms against her sides so she wouldn't hurt herself.

"Amy! They don't know who I am!" he said. "It was too dark for Rommel to see what I really look like. I'll say my sister left it there or something."

Dan wasn't sure she had heard him, which was probably lucky for Jake. His plan would not have worked. The back of the watch was engraved with Amy's name, cell phone number, and e-mail.

Dan leaned forward and put his hand on Amy's shoulder. "We stole a Caravaggio," he said. "We shouldn't have any problem stealing something that actually belongs to us."

Amy looked at him and blinked several times as if she didn't know where she was.

"The watch. The diamond," she said hoarsely, and turned her head toward the dashboard clock.

They all followed her gaze.

"Maybe Vesper One will give us an extension," Jake said.

No one bothered to answer him.

"I shouldn't have turned the lights out," Atticus said.

"If you hadn't they would have found the fake diamond," Amy said dully.

"Let me see it," Dan said to distract himself. Something was nagging him and he wanted to think of anything except what was happening to the hostages.

Who will die? Uncle Alistair? Nellie?

Amy pulled the velvet bag out of her pocket and tossed it over her shoulder.

"We'll get your watch back," Jake quietly reassured Amy again. "I know it was important to you."

"I know what set the metal detector off," Dan said. "It wasn't the diamond; it was the velvet bag. The inside is lined with some kind of metallic cloth."

"Why would they—"

The Vesper phone buzzed, silencing everyone. Amy had to dig through her strewn gear to find it. Her voice shook as she read the text aloud.

Thank you for your help at the Pergamon.
We could not have done it without you,

but I must apologize pro meus valde delictum. And you must now find it. Your friends are all alive . . . for now. Off to Timbuktu you go. No margin for error. If you fail to recover the transgression within 48 hours, I will flip a coin. Heads for Phoenix. Tails for Oh.

Vesper One

Stunned disbelief filled the car. Another minute ticked by before anyone could speak.

"The hostages are safe," Amy finally said, a fresh flood of tears running down her face.

Dan let out a deep breath. He couldn't take it in. His stomach felt misplaced, as if he were suspended on top of a roller coaster. "What does he mean by *our help* at the Pergamon?"

"Vesper sarcasm?" Atticus said.

"Maybe," Dan answered. "Why would Vesper One apologize for a valid delectable prom menu?"

"'Apologize *pro meus valde delictum*,'" Atticus said, pronouncing the words correctly. "It's Latin. It means apologize 'for my great transgression.'"

"Apology not accepted," Dan said.

And for the first time in a while, everyone laughed.

Jake called his father's travel agent, who specialized in journeys to remote places. The good news was that the Berlin airport had reopened after the snowstorm and flights were landing and taking off. The bad news was that Timbuktu was one of most difficult places in the world to reach.

"We can't get there from here," Jake said, after he got off the phone. "At least not very quickly. There's a flight out of Berlin tomorrow morning, but it doesn't get into Bamako in Mali until late tomorrow evening."

"Bamako?" Dan said. "Mali? I thought we were going to Timbuktu."

"Timbuktu and Bamako are in the country of Mali. To get to Timbuktu, you have to go to Bamako first. The problem is getting from Bamako to Timbuktu," Jake continued. "There are only three flights a week, and the next flight isn't for two days."

"We could rent a car," Amy said. "Or hire a driver."

"Nine hours across the desert," Jake said. "If you don't have a breakdown, which happens about seventy percent of the time. The other way to Timbuktu is by ferry. But it's a three-day trip if the ferries are in operation, which half the time they aren't."

"Too bad we don't have Jonah's private jet," Dan said.

"That's brilliant!" Amy said. "Why can't we use his jet while they're in Pompeii? The jet could be here in a few hours."

"And we wouldn't have to worry about getting through security," Atticus added.

"I'll text Erasmus," Amy said, typing quickly into her phone.

"What about your watch?" Dan asked.

Amy took a deep breath. "We have to get it back. If we can't do it before we leave, we'll come back after we finish in Timbuktu. We don't have a choice. In the meantime, we'll check into a hotel and get a few hours' sleep."

"Room service!" Dan and Atticus shouted in unison.

They checked into connecting suites at the Brandenburger Hof, not far from the Pergamon Museum. Each suite had two bedrooms with canopied king-sized beds. The bedrooms had attached master bathrooms equipped with steam and sauna rooms, and flat-screen televisions everywhere. There was even one you could see from the toilet.

"It's a perfect design," Dan said as they toured the rooms.

"A little over the top," Amy said.

Atticus opened the well-stocked minibar and started liberating chips, soda pop, mixed nuts, and candy. Jake picked up the television remote and began channel surfing for news about the Pergamon.

"I'm going to call Evan and then take a shower," Amy said, handing Dan the Vesper satellite phone and her own cell phone. "Erasmus should be calling back. Tell him what's going on. And charge both phones. When we get to Timbuktu we'll have to hit the ground running. We'll need all of our batteries topped up."

"What about your laptop?"

"I'll charge it in the other room."

Dan grinned. "Give Evan a virtual kiss from me."

Amy glanced at Jake and felt her face redden. He was still flipping through the channels and didn't appear to be paying attention. *Why do I care?* She closed the door to the second suite.

After the door clicked shut, Jake turned to Dan. "How serious is it between Amy and Evan?"

Dan started humming Mendelssohn's "Wedding March," then put his index finger into his mouth like he was gagging.

Room service finally answered. "I need . . . uh . . . do you speak English? Hang on." He waved Atticus over to the phone. "Can you order everything on the menu?"

"Everything?"

"You can skip any kind of vegetable matter."

Atticus took the phone and started going down the menu from the top.

Amy broke into a broad grin when Evan appeared on the screen.

"I wasn't sure you'd be there," she said.

"Kind of hard to head home when your girlfriend is robbing a museum. Are you okay?"

Amy managed a wobbly smile. "I'm fine, but we didn't get the Jubilee." She went on to explain what had happened in the Pergamon, leaving out her SUV fit.

As she spoke Evan typed notes into the comm center database. When she finished, he read over what he had written and asked her questions to make sure he had it right.

"Sorry about that," he said. "But the only way to identify Vesper One and figure out where the hostages are is to sluice information until something pops to the surface. Erasmus is double-checking the data. Vesper One will make a mistake. Data mining always works."

"I hope so," Amy said.

"E-mail me a photo of that velvet bag," Evan said. "Maybe we can find out who manufactured it. It shouldn't be too hard to run it down with the metallic lining. Why would it even *have* metallic lining?"

"I have no idea," Amy said. "But I wish I'd taken the fake diamond out of it."

"By what you said about the security, and Vanek

showing up, it sounds like the heist wouldn't have worked anyway. You were lucky to get out of there."

Amy shuddered. "Without Jake they would have had us."

Evan frowned.

"What's the matter?"

"I'm just tired. I've been trying to figure out if someone's feeding information to Vesper One."

Amy felt her stomach twist. "Do you still think it's Ian?" she asked quietly, praying that Evan would tell her it'd all been a mistake. She couldn't believe that Ian would betray them. That he'd betray *her*.

Evan pressed his lips together, then spoke slowly. "Ian is still our number one suspect, but there's no proof that he's working for Vesper One other than his odd behavior. It would be unfair to openly accuse him at this point, and maybe even damaging. When he's here he's been a big help. We need him."

"Do you still think our data is compromised?"

"It's hard to say. I'm monitoring it twenty-four-seven and haven't detected any intruders, but that doesn't mean that there isn't a mole."

"Call me if you have any updates. Day or night. It doesn't matter." Amy glanced away from the screen, then looked back shyly. "You can call me anytime . . . for any reason. I really miss you, Evan."

"I miss you, too, Ames." Evan took a deep breath. "Are you sure everything is okay?"

"I guess. I mean . . ."

"You and Jake seem to be getting along pretty well."

Amy felt her face flush again, but this time with anger. "What do you mean by that?"

"Nothing," Evan said. "I was just—"

"It's getting late," Amy said, looking at her watch—which wasn't there, adding to her frustration. "I better go." She ended the call and closed her laptop. The *last* thing she needed right now was to worry about Evan's ridiculous concerns. She sighed. Why did everything have to be so completely confusing?

Evan stared at his reflection in the blank monitor and saw that his mouth was hanging open. Why would Amy react so strongly to a simple question? He'd only asked because the last time they'd talked, she said Jake was being a jerk. He was about to try to reconnect with her, but was interrupted by a scream.

He jumped up and looked around for some kind of weapon, but all he could find was a Ping-Pong paddle. He grabbed it and rushed downstairs.

Ian Kabra was standing in the living room with blood running down his face.

"Sorry to disturb your game," Ian said, looking at the paddle.

Evan clenched his teeth. "I wasn't playing Ping-Pong," Evan said, hiding the paddle behind his back. "What happened?"

"Saladin happened. Grace's mangy cat. When I

walked in he jumped on my head like a puma. He nearly took my ear off!"

Saladin was lying comfortably in an expensive chair, grooming Kabra blood off his front paws.

"Don't just stand there," Ian said. "Go fetch the first-aid kit. I believe it's in the kitchen."

"Where have you been?" Evan asked.

"Out, obviously. How about that first-aid kit?"

"Go *fetch* it yourself."

"I'm wounded," Ian huffed.

"It's worse than you think." Evan pointed at one of Ian's expensive, handmade shoes. On the toe was an egg-size glob of gray goo.

"What is it?" Ian shouted in horror.

"Looks like a fur ball to me." Evan started back upstairs, wondering if Saladin could detect something in Ian that Evan couldn't prove. *Perhaps Saladin is trying to catch a rat*, he thought.

Ian kicked the slimy fur ball off his shoe. It hit the wall above the sofa with a sickening splat and slid down like a giant slug.

He has some nerve, Ian thought as he watched Evan disappear up the stairs. Sure, his computer skills kept him from being *completely* useless, but Evan wasn't a Cahill and needed to show some respect for the world's most powerful family.

Amy could really do better, he thought as he backed

his way into the kitchen, afraid to take his eyes off the demonic cat. When he got there, he closed the door and latched it behind him.

What does that beast have against me? Animals had always taken a shine to Ian, from the homing poodles on the Kabra estate, to his imported polo ponies, Sebastian and Quigley. American cats were clearly terrible judges of character.

All Ian had wanted to do when he dragged himself into the Attleboro mansion was lie down on the sofa and take a nap. Now, he had to stem the flow of blood and figure out a way to get the lion out of the living room. He found the first-aid kit and patched his ear as best he could, then took a dish towel and buffed the slime off his shoe. He badly missed his servants.

Now for my nemesis. He opened a cupboard stacked high with tins of red snapper. As soon as he started the electric can opener, there was a scratching at the door. He opened it very carefully. The Egyptian Mau slipped through the crack and strutted over to the cat dish like he was Tutankhamen entering a banquet hall.

Mrrp, said Saladin before starting in on his fishy meal.

"Just remember who fed you," Ian said. He shut the door, walked back to the living room, arranged the pillow, and lay down on his good ear, hoping Saladin didn't know how to open a latch.

Dan was also eating fish when Amy's cell phone rang.

"Heffo?" He tried to swallow a mouthful of *bratfisch mit pommes frites* and started choking. "Hong on." He reached for a glass of ice water and took a deep gulp. "Sorry. Who's this?"

"Erasmus," a deep voice replied.

"Hey. How's Pompeii? How are Hamilton and Jonah? I hear Mount Vesuvius is about ready to blow!"

"I wouldn't know," Erasmus said. "We're in Mumbai."

"As in India? I thought you were in Italy."

"We came across Luna Amato in Pompeii early this morning," Erasmus said. "This is where she led us. Where's Amy?"

"She's taking a shower."

"Tell her Jonah's jet is on the way. The pilot will call you when it lands in Berlin."

"I will, but —"

"Gotta go." Erasmus ended the call.

"Nice talking to you, too," Dan said and exchanged the phone for a *pomme frite*, aka French fry, because Atticus had scarfed down the last piece of *bratfisch*, aka deep-fried fish, while he was talking to Erasmus.

"Here it is!" Jake said. He had found something on the television about the Pergamon blackout.

Dan and Atticus joined him in front of the tube. A news reporter was interviewing Rommel outside the entrance to the museum.

"The reporter's asking him if there was anything

stolen from the museum," Atticus translated. "Rommel says that the collection is all accounted for except for an old manuscript called *The Book of Ingenious Devices*. He says that the manuscript may have been moved by one of the curators. He hasn't had a chance to talk to all the staff yet."

"It's been swiped," Dan said. "Or more accurately, it's *being* swiped." He pointed at the screen.

Cheyenne and Casper Wyoming were walking right past where Rommel was being interviewed. They smiled at the camera. Casper had a wrapped bundle under his arm the size of a large book.

"Vesper used us!" Dan said. "The Golden Jubilee was a diversion!" He pulled the velvet bag out of his pocket. "He knew this would set off the metal detector. He probably tipped Milos Vanek off, too. And then the Wyomings grabbed the book, which isn't nearly as valuable as some of the other stuff they have in there. There probably wasn't even a guard on it!" He picked up the Vesper phone and read part of the text again, aloud: "'Thank you for your help at the Pergamon. We could not have done it without you.'"

Jake stood up. "I've had enough of the Vespers for tonight. I'm going to sleep." He walked into one of the bedrooms and closed the door.

Atticus yawned. "I think I'll go to sleep, too." He snagged his third dessert from the serving cart and took it into another bedroom with him.

Dan switched the television off and slumped into a

chair. He couldn't sleep. There was a secret itching at him, scratching away at the back of his brain until he felt like he was going crazy.

Dan took his cell phone out and stared at his last text exchange with AJT—the person who was either posing as Arthur Trent . . . or was actually Dan and Amy's father.

If you're really my dad, can you tell me what special thing you said to make us smile together?

The answer had come back lightning fast.

Moon face.

Aside from Amy, the only person who could know this special nickname was his father.

Dan had deleted all of the previous texts from AJT, swearing that he would not contact him again. But he couldn't help himself. He glanced at Amy's door, then quickly thumbed in a text.

Why did you set us up at Pergamon Museum? What is The Book of Ingenious Devices?

Dan stared at the screen. An hour went by, then two. He finally dozed off, waiting for a reply from the dead.

CHAPTER 12

The hostages were waiting on the dead as well. The Vesper guards had watched the whole thing unfold on their video monitors. Reagan Holt had died from an apparent heart attack on the ninth one-handed push-up of her third set.

At first they thought she was just resting, but the boy named Phoenix rushed over and shook her.

"Reagan?" Phoenix looked at the others with grim horror. "She's not moving."

"Ridiculous!" Alistair Oh said. He joined Phoenix and carefully turned her over. Reagan's face was blue. "Oh, my God!" he shouted.

The guards watched as a few of the hostages took turns administering CPR, while the others shouted for a doctor until they were all hoarse. They cried. Finally, they covered Reagan with a sheet and left her by the door.

The guards waited to go down until after they finished their poker game. Before opening the door, they pulled balaclavas over their heads and shouted for everyone to back away.

The hostages looked at them dully, spent with grief. One of the guards pointed a camera at them. The other pointed a pistol.

"Why don't you just shoot us right now?" Fiske asked. "Get it over with."

The man with the camera laughed. "I *am* shooting you . . . in high definition."

"Pigs!" Nellie said.

"Cretins!" Natalie hissed.

The man shoved the pistol into his waistband and grabbed Reagan's arms roughly. But before he could drag the corpse an inch, Reagan's lifeless legs did an acrobatic curl, latching on to his thick neck in a scissor lock. A split second later he was flying through the air, slamming onto the concrete floor on his back. The supposedly dead girl and the others swarmed him and his partner like a pack of flying monkeys. The other Vesper guard managed to land a vicious kick to the knee of the man called Alistair, but it did no good. The guards were overwhelmed.

Reagan picked up the gun and the camera. She put the camera an inch from his face. "Now I'm shooting *you* in high definition!" she cried, then dropped the camera on his chest.

The guard tried to respond, but didn't have enough air in his lungs to speak. His partner was unconscious. The hostages helped the old man he had kicked to his feet. They filed through the concrete door, sliding it closed with a loud *bang*.

CHAPTER 13

Cheyenne Wyoming was running a brush through her long blond hair on a private jet flying south at thirty-five thousand feet. Her twin brother, Casper, sat across from her holding a small mirror and a pair of sharp tweezers, picking errant blond hairs from his nose.

"I told you that if we pulled off the heist at the Pergamon, we'd be back in with Vesper One," Casper said. "Ouch!" He held the tweezers up, looking at his harvest.

"We're not back in," Cheyenne said. "We're just not dead. Yet." She picked up her smartphone and read Vesper One's text aloud.

The wolves are at bay . . . for now. But it will take only the slightest irritation for me to set them upon you again. Proceed immediately to Bamako. From there you'll catch the ship to Timbuktu. Keep an eye on the Cahills,

but do not impede them in any way. Unless
you want my pack of assassins to tear
you to shreds.

Vesper One

"Guy has a way with words," Casper said. "But he makes mistakes."

"Like what?"

"Like failing to take Danny Boy as a hostage. His big sister wouldn't try any tricks if Vesper One had her little brother."

"He's turned it to his advantage," Cheyenne said. "The boy's pretty bright."

"He's not bright," Casper said. "He's lucky." He pulled the last nose hair out. "Ouch!"

CHAPTER 14

Dan was dreaming that Vesper One was calling him. . . .

"Where's my phone?"

His eyes shot open. Amy was standing in front of him in a hotel bathrobe, her hands on her hips.

"Uh . . ." He looked down at his cell phone and realized that the ringing he'd heard wasn't a dream.

"Never mind," Amy said. "I see it. It's probably Evan." She picked it up. "Hello?" She hesitated. "Who is this?"

A look of shock crossed her face.

"I'm betting it's not your boyfriend," Dan said.

Amy shook her head and put the phone on speaker.

"How did you get this number?" she asked.

"Interpol is the largest international police organization in the world. But that is not how I got your number. Is your brother, Dan, there? I believe he has a wallet that belongs to me, and a priceless manuscript belonging to the Pergamon Museum."

"Yep on the first one," Dan said. "Nope on the second. We didn't swipe *The Book of Ingenious Devices*."

"Then how do you know it is missing?"

"Television." Dan glanced at Amy. "Hang on a sec, Vanek." He took her phone and put it on mute. "You missed some things during your Skype date with Evan."

"It wasn't much of a date," Amy said.

Dan quickly filled her in, then took her phone off mute. "Sorry about that, Vanek. We're on an airplane and they're telling us to switch off our phones. We'll have to continue this conversation late—"

"Another of your funny jokes," Vanek interrupted. "You are in rooms three thirteen and three fourteen of the Brandenburger Hof. I am standing outside your door, and all of the exits from the hotel, as you say in America, are covered. So as not to disturb the other guests I would like you to come out quietly."

Dan and Amy turned and stared at the door in disbelief.

"We need to think about it." Dan put the phone back on mute and walked over to the door. He looked through the peephole. A distorted Agent Vanek was looking back at him with a cell phone to his ear.

Amy walked over and resolutely opened the door.

Milos Vanek looked at the two children. They looked exhausted, disheveled, and nervous. The girl wore a white hotel bathrobe, and her hair was tangled as if she had just awoken. The boy looked like he had slept in his clothes.

"May I come in?" He wasn't really asking, but it was always best to be civil. He had the hotel surrounded with plainclothes policemen, but he wanted to remove the Cahills quietly if possible.

Amy nodded and stepped aside. He slipped past her and Dan into the elegant room.

"Very posh," he said. "It must be nice to have more money than you know what to do with."

"We slept in a graveyard the night before," Dan said.

Vanek smiled. Apparently, the boy's imagination knew no bounds. He looked at Amy. "You will need to dress. And if you are thinking of exiting through the door of the other suite, I have a policeman stationed outside that door."

Dan's face cracked. "You don't understand what's going on here."

Vanek looked at him. "I understand very well. The theft of a priceless masterpiece, escape from jail, assault of a police officer, impersonating a police officer, pickpocketing." He held his hand out. "I would like my wallet and passport back . . . and my keys."

"How did you get my cell phone number?" the girl asked.

"You left it for me at the Pergamon Museum," Vanek said. He reached into his pocket and pulled out her watch. "Perhaps not intentionally."

The children stared at the watch in dismay. The girl put her hand out tentatively.

Vanek shook his head and put the watch behind his back. "The wallet," he said.

"Then what?" the boy asked.

"Then I will arrest you and take you to jail."

"We didn't take anything from the Pergamon!"

"That remains to be seen. And there is still the priceless Caravaggio painting you stole in Italy."

"Which was a fake," Dan reminded him. "We should have gotten a reward for returning the real one."

"The wallet," Vanek repeated.

The boy crossed his arms over his chest and shook his head. "No."

"Dan," the girl said sweetly, giving her brother a meaningful glance. "You know that watch has sentimental value to me."

"I know," the boy said, returning her look. "But Vanek's wallet has *practical* value to him. If he lets us go, I'll give him the wallet."

The boy was correct. The wallet did have practical value to Vanek, which is why he had entered the room alone rather than having the door kicked in by the backup team in the lobby. The museum guards knew the boy had handcuffed him to the stanchion, so there was no getting around that embarrassment. But no one knew the boy had also stolen his wallet. Still, Vanek shook his head.

"No deal," he said.

"Fine," the boy said. "Let's skip the watch and wallet and go directly to jail. Call your guys up here and search the rooms. You'll never find the wallet."

"I was hoping we could do this discreetly," Vanek said, calling his bluff. He took a two-way radio out of his pocket.

"Wait!" the boy said, his face pale as snow.

Vanek frowned. The two children looked so sad and exhausted. There was none of the pleading or bravado he'd so often seen when crimes caught up with the guilty.

"How about this for a deal?" Dan asked. "I'll give you your wallet back for the watch." He hesitated. "And if you let us go, I'll give you Luna Amato."

The very sound of her name brought an angry flush to Vanek's face. Thieves, murderers, forgers—they were all bad. But the worst of all of them was a dirty cop. When he'd reported Luna to his superiors, he'd been met by blank looks, blustering, and once even a cold glimpse of terror. Somehow she had gotten to them. Vanek had determined to track her himself, but after Turkey her trail had gone completely cold. He had been hunting Luna when he'd received an anonymous tip about the Cahills being at the Pergamon.

"You know where she is?" he asked.

Dan met his eyes. "I do. But I won't tell you if you arrest us."

Vanek locked eyes with the defiant boy, weighing his choices.

"How can I trust you will tell me the truth?"

"How can I trust that you won't send your men crashing in here after I tell you where she is?"

"You have my promise," Vanek said.

"And you have my promise."

Vanek stared at him for several seconds. The boy did not blink. He could find the Cahill children whenever he wanted. The same could not be said for Luna Amato.

"I know there is more to what you are doing than meets my eye," he said. "I am in a position to help you if you would allow me."

The girl shook her head. "We can't do that." Vanek could hear the effort it cost to keep her voice steady. Something nagged him about the children. Something about them didn't fit with the crimes he knew they had committed.

Vanek paused for an agonizing second, then brought the watch out from behind his back. The girl's face crumpled for just an instant, as if the relief of having it back was almost more than her slim body could bear. The boy nodded, then reached into his back pocket and pulled the wallet out.

Vanek smiled. "Hidden in plain sight, I see." He took the wallet. "Where is Luna Amato?"

"Mumbai."

"I was stationed in Mumbai for many years. It is a very big city. Twenty million people. Where can I find her among them?"

"Find Jonah Wizard and you'll find Luna Amato."

Vanek raised an eyebrow. "Jonah Wizard, the star of music and the films? What does he have to do with the lying, traitorous Luna Amato?"

"He's keeping an eye on her."

"For what purpose?"

Amy cut in. "That's not part of the deal," she said. "Do you have police stationed at all the exits?"

Vanek nodded. "I have your promise about Luna Amato?" he countered.

The boy looked at him. "As Jonah Wizard would say, *word*."

CHAPTER 15

"Word." Jonah Wizard shoved his cell phone back in his pocket and looked at Hamilton Holt. "That was Amy. They're borrowing the jet for a trek to Timbuktu. The jewel snatch was a bust, but the hostages are still okay. Some Interpol dude is bouncing in from Deutschland to check out Luna."

Hamilton stared at his hip-hop mega-platinum-star partner in confusion. He'd been with Jonah 24/7 for several days and he understood the Mumbaiya slang the food vendor was jabbering to them better than he understood his famous cousin.

"Are you saying that they're using your jet to get to Timbuktu, and they didn't get the Jubilee Diamond, but Reagan and the other hostages are okay?"

"You need subtitles, brother?"

"I guess." Hamilton took the banana leaf topped with *pav bhaji* from the vendor and snapped open his can of Thums Up soda. Across the street a snake charmer was coaxing a king cobra out of a basket with a flute.

"Snakes are deaf," Jonah said,

"I hear you, man," Hamilton said.

"No, they really are deaf," Jonah said. "That cobra can't hear a note from that flute. See how the charmer bobs and weaves? The snake's mirroring the dude's movements, not shuffling to the music." He crossed the street, dropped some cash in the snake charmer's money basket, then started bobbing and weaving along with the charmer.

Erasmus had insisted they travel to India completely incognito. No paparazzi. No limos. They were getting around the vast city on motorcycles. Well . . . Erasmus had a motorcycle. He had gotten them a motorcycle rickshaw. One drove, one rode, which was a constant source of bickering.

Also, no five-star hotels. They were staying in a Madrigal safe house, which was more like a shack.

No five-star restaurants, either. Hamilton took another bite of his *pav bhaji* as he watched his cousin.

No Jonah Wizard.

"There can't be any sightings of Jonah in the country," Erasmus had said. "We can't tail Luna if we're being tailed."

They had followed Luna to an airport outside Rome, where she booked a first-class seat to Mumbai. Erasmus booked a trio of coach seats near the back restrooms. It was the first time Jonah had ever flown in coach, and he was not amused by the whole concept of a middle seat.

When the flight landed, Hamilton and Jonah grabbed what little gear they had and hopped up, eager to get off the plane so they didn't lose Luna in the crowd.

"Sit down," Erasmus had said. "She has to get her bags and get through passport control and customs. That will take one hour and twelve minutes. It will take us sixteen minutes to be at the curb. We don't have bags, and I know a guy in passport control."

Sixteen minutes later they stepped out of the Mumbai airport. It took Erasmus thirty minutes to procure the motorcycle and the rickshaw. Exactly twenty-six minutes later, Luna Amato walked out of the terminal and climbed into the back of a limo.

Their plan was to stake out Luna Amato's hotel in six-hour shifts. Erasmus had insisted Hamilton and Jonah watch the hotel together so they could keep each other awake. When Jonah asked who was going to keep *him* awake, Erasmus answered that he didn't sleep. As far as they could tell, it was the truth.

Hamilton washed his last bite down with a gulp of Thums Up as Jonah came back from his cobra dance.

"We need to relieve Erasmus," Ham said, looking at his watch.

"We also need to tell him about that Interpol dude," Jonah said.

"What Interpol dude?" Hamilton asked, following him to the rickshaw.

"Weren't you listening? Milos Vanek is coming to

town. We gotta find out what's cracking with Lune dawg. My turn to drive."

They found Erasmus leaning against a wall across the street from Luna's hotel, in the exact same spot he had been leaning several hours earlier. He wasn't worried that the hotel had several exits that Luna could slip through. His extended family was a fixture in the hotel/hospitality industry. A single phone call had put dozens of eyes on Luna, monitoring every move she made. If she took a single step out of the hotel, Erasmus would know about it.

"Yo," Jonah said.

"Hey, Erasmus," Hamilton said.

Erasmus gave them a nod, then swung onto his motorcycle. "See you in a few hours."

Jonah and Hamilton watched after him long after he had disappeared into the throng of traffic.

Erasmus did not drive to the safe house. In fact, he hadn't been inside since he'd arrived with Hamilton and Jonah. Instead he drove to a cyber café. There were hundreds of them in Mumbai, and he never went to the same one twice.

He walked in, paid his fee, and found a terminal away from the windows in the darkest corner. He logged on and opened his encrypted e-mail account. There were over five hundred unread e-mails. Cahills from all over the world were feeding information to

Attleboro. In turn, Evan forwarded everything, no matter how trivial, to Erasmus. Somewhere in all of this data, Vesper One had left a trail, a single cyber fingerprint they could use to track him down. The Vespers usually operated in the dark, but by taking the hostages and killing McIntyre, they had scurried briefly into the light. This was the time to find them.

Erasmus pored through all the e-mails, but only two items stood out. Thieves had broken into the Laboratoire National des Champs Magnétiques Intenses in Toulouse, France, and stolen all of their electromagnets. All of them. It had taken the entire weekend to get the equipment out of the laboratory. Unless the thieves were particle physicists, they would have absolutely no use for their loot.

The other item was a brief mention that a replica of the Antikythera Mechanism had been stolen from the American Computer Museum in Bozeman, Montana. The original device had been recovered from a Mediterranean shipwreck by a Greek sponge diver in 1900, but was believed to have been constructed between 150 and 100 B.C. At first, it was thought to be one of the first forms of a mechanized clock. Now it was considered to be world's oldest-known analog computer. No one knew exactly what the device had been used for, but scientists believed the mechanism could track the Metonic calendar, predict solar eclipses, and calculate the timing of the ancient Olympic Games.

The replica was beautiful, but what interested

Erasmus was the photograph of the original Antikythera fragment. It looked familiar to him, though he couldn't quite recall where he had seen it before.

He memorized every detail of the fragment before dragging it into the Vesper thumb drive. The fragment was just one of thousands of pieces. Eventually, the pieces would all click together to form a prison cell for the Vespers.

His final task was to Google Jonah Wizard. Jonah had been very good about not being the world-famous Jonah Wizard the past few days, but Erasmus knew it couldn't last. Jonah's fans were on the lookout, with reports coming in that he'd been spotted in Alice Springs, Australia, rapping with aboriginal people, then in Churchill, Canada, getting down with polar bears. One particularly oddball rumor placed him in

Manaus, Brazil, searching for El Dorado. And the next had him in—Mumbai, India. Erasmus hit the link, which led him to a YouTube video of Jonah Wizard dancing with a king cobra.

This is going to complicate things, Erasmus thought.

When the video ended, he put in a second thumb drive, which completely wiped the computer's hard drive. While it worked, he looked at his watch. He had just enough time to get something to eat and catch a movie. Perhaps a double feature. He loved Hindi-language films, and what better place to watch one than the birthplace of Bollywood?

The computer's alarm woke Vesper Three, which meant that data was streaming in. Erasmus was online again. It had been so easy to swap out his thumb drive with one Vesper Three had made. While Erasmus thought he was wiping the memory from the computers he used, he was actually transferring every bit of data and every keystroke to Vesper Three.

Like taking candy from a baby. The Cahills have no idea who they're dealing with.

Vesper Three flashed forward to the shock on Amy's face when she discovered that one of her own had betrayed her. The Vespers were closer than Amy thought; so close they used her little command clubhouse as a base of their own. The so-called Cahill leader thought her mansion was safe. But the Vespers had eyes—and agents—everywhere.

Vesper Three smiled. *It's about time for Luna Amato to make her move. The rats are all gathered and sniffing the trap.*

Vesper Three e-mailed the signal to release the bait.

CHAPTER 16

"This way!"

"No, this way!"

"You're both wrong. This way!"

"Everybody just shut up!" Ted shouted.

This stopped everyone in their tracks. Ted Starling rarely spoke and never shouted. The hostages had raced through a long, dimly lit tunnel and were now standing in front of three branches that snaked off into three different directions.

"You're making too much noise," Ted said. "The two guards we locked in the bunker aren't the only ones here! I heard five distinct voices. With the two guards locked in the bunker, that means there are at least seven people down here. Probably more."

Nellie had been holding Ted's arm, guiding him through the tunnel. "Ted's right," she said. "We're out of the bunker, but we're still trapped."

"Maybe we should split up," Reagan suggested.

"I don't think that's a good idea," Fiske said. "The only advantage we have is our number."

"No, it isn't," Reagan said. "We have this." She pulled the guard's pistol from her waistband.

"I hope we won't need that," Fiske said.

Ted felt the walls. "Tell me what it looks like down here."

"We're in a rock tunnel," Nellie answered. "It might be an old mine. There's a lightbulb about every thirty feet, covered by a rusty metal sconce. Some of the bulbs are out. We've passed a couple of metal doors, but they were rusted closed. In front of us are three identical tunnels, left, right, and straight ahead."

"Are there markings on the walls that say where we are or what this place is?" Ted asked.

"Nothing."

"Put me in front of the three tunnels and let me listen for a moment without anybody talking."

Nellie positioned him, and Ted frowned in concentration.

"There are people walking down the right-hand tunnel. I think they're a few minutes away, which means that this underground warren is humongous. They're not running, which means they probably don't know we've escaped. I don't get anything from the middle tunnel. But there's definitely fresh air coming out of the tunnel on the left."

"Then it's left," Alistair said.

"Let's get out of here!" Reagan said, bounding ahead of the others.

Natalie followed with Fiske, Nellie led Ted, and

Phoenix and limping Alistair brought up the rear. The guard's kick had badly damaged Alistair's knee, and Phoenix's shoulder was almost the right height for Alistair to lean against.

They hurried on and on, Alistair hobbling as fast as he could. The tunnel seemed endless and each noise or bump had the group whipping their heads around in fear. By Nellie's calculation, it was almost a half a mile to the end. Reagan had outpaced everyone and was waiting for them with a blank expression when they arrived.

"It's a dead end," she said.

"You're joking," Nellie said.

"I wish." Reagan turned and slapped the wall. "It's solid rock."

"Shh." Ted pressed his ear up to the rock. "They're coming!" he said.

"Stand behind me," Alistair said to Phoenix.

"There's fresh air!" Ted had his pale face pointed at the ceiling. "I can feel it! Where's it coming from?"

They had been so busy looking for breaks in the rock wall in front of them, no one had bothered to check the ceiling. Above them was a narrow shaft with dim light filtering through the opening.

"If I get a good jump I can reach the ladder!" Reagan took a running start and sprang up, just managing to catch the bottom rung with her good arm. She pulled herself through the opening like an Olympic gymnast on a parallel bar, then dropped back to the ground.

"There's a grate. It's twenty-five feet up, max. Let's go!"

They boosted Phoenix up first, followed by Alistair, Ted, Natalie, and Fiske.

Reagan cupped her hands to give Nellie a boost to the bottom rung.

"What about you?" Nellie asked.

"I'll jump," Reagan said. "But first I'm going to slow our friends down."

Nellie shook her head. "It's not safe. Get out of here and let me do the honors. I'm pretty good with a gun."

"I don't have to hit anyone," Reagan insisted. "I'll fire a few rounds down the tunnel and let the ricochet and noise do the rest. Besides, you can't jump high enough to reach the bottom rung."

Reluctantly, Nellie put her foot into Reagan's cupped hands and grabbed the bottom rung. Her shoulder wound reopened and it felt like someone had splashed it with gasoline and set it on fire. Nellie gritted her teeth and ignored the pain and the warm blood trickling down her side.

Seven deafening gun blasts reverberated through the shaft, followed by a barrage of return fire, almost causing Nellie to lose her grip. "Are you okay?" Nellie shouted down.

"I'm fine," Reagan replied. "Keep moving."

Nellie tried to climb higher, but the line above her had come to a complete stop.

"Hurry!" she shouted.

"The grate's padlocked!" Phoenix shouted back.

Reagan scrambled up behind Nellie like a monkey and handed her the pistol. "There's one round left. Pass it up and tell Phoenix to make it count and to hurry. The Vespers will be here any second!"

"Have you ever fired a pistol?" Alistair asked Phoenix as he gingerly handed over the gun.

Phoenix gave him a weak smile. "Kind of," he said. "I was on the film set of *Gangsta Kronikles* with Jonah. They let me shoot a pistol, but it shot blanks."

"Hurry it up!" Reagan shouted. "They're almost here!"

Phoenix pointed the pistol at the lock, turned his head away, and pulled the trigger.

Click.

"Safety!" Reagan shouted. "It's on the left side by your thumb! Flick it up!"

Phoenix flicked the safety and pulled the trigger again.

Boom!

A piece of shrapnel sliced open Phoenix's right hand. He instinctively jerked it off the rung, causing him to wobble, and then to start to fall. Alistair's firm hand smacked into his back, stopping him from falling.

"You've got to get the grate open!"

But the grate was heavy, and Phoenix couldn't lift it. They could all hear the pounding of the guards' feet now. Natalie gave a frantic look below her, then clambered over the top of Ted to give Phoenix and Alistair a hand. It took several precious seconds before the heavy steel grate finally slapped open. The hostages piled out quickly. As Reagan hoisted herself out of the shaft, bullets whizzed through the opening. She slammed to the ground and rolled away.

"Close," she said, looking at a smoking rip in her coveralls where a bullet had grazed her.

They were in a small clearing surrounded by giant fir trees. It was sweltering hot, but they didn't care. For the first time in weeks, they filled their lungs with fresh air.

"Which way?" Natalie asked.

"That way." Reagan pointed. "Downhill. You're bound to run into a road or a river."

"What do you mean by *you're*?" Nellie asked, giving Reagan a suspicious look.

"No offense to any of you, but you're not going to make very good time," Reagan said. "Someone has to hang here and keep these gophers in their hole. Don't worry. I'll catch up with you."

"You're out of bullets," Alistair reminded her.

Reagan picked up a large rock. "Ammo!" She hurtled the rock down the opening and they heard a satisfying grunt of pain.

"I'm staying with you," Nellie said, then turned to the others. "Go, hurry!"

Fiske took Ted's arm. "We'll see you downhill somewhere," he said, and the group made for the trees, Alistair limping behind him.

CHAPTER 17

Reagan and Nellie were rolling two rather large boulders toward the opening when the dogs attacked them.

Reagan saw the two pit bulls streaking across the clearing first.

"Don't move!" she shouted to Nellie.

But Nellie had already thrown a stick at the dog heading toward her. Unfortunately, the only thing the pit bull was interested in fetching was Nellie. It knocked her down and bit viciously into her leg.

Several heavily armed guards wearing balaclavas came running out of the woods. One of the guards called the dog off before turning on Reagan.

"Stay where you are!" Reagan pointed the pistol at them.

The guards only laughed.

"I mean it!" Reagan said.

"I can count," the guard said. "You're on empty." He raised his rifle.

Reagan dropped the pistol and rushed over to Nellie.

"How bad is it?" a shaken Nellie asked.

The dog had bitten her face as well as her leg.

"We need a doctor!" Reagan shouted.

"You're not going to get one," the guard said. "Where are the others?"

"They went back down the shaft," Reagan lied.

He shook his head before turning to his colleagues. "Send the dogs out. They'll find them."

The remaining hostages had only gone a mile and a half, most of it downhill, and Alistair was already exhausted.

"I hear water," Ted said.

"How far?" Fiske asked.

"It's close."

"It's right here!" Natalie said.

They joined her at the edge of a deep precipice. Two hundred feet below was a roaring river.

"It looks as if there's a trail all the way to the bottom," Natalie said. "But it's narrow and slippery. We should wait for Reagan and Nellie before we attempt it."

Fiske considered it, but only for a second. "No. We better go."

He took a step out and started down the cliff.

Reagan and Nellie had been flex-cuffed and pushed into the back of a windowless panel truck.

Nellie swallowed. "Is it really bad?" Her white and

black hair was matted to her head with sweat and blood.

Reagan examined her in the dim light. "Your face is a little swollen, but I don't think it's serious. I'm more concerned about your leg. We need to get the wounds cleaned up so they don't get infected."

"I shouldn't have thrown the stick," Nellie said.

"It's pretty hard not to when a vicious animal is charging you. I learned about it in survival school. Predators expect their prey to run away or defend themselves. When that doesn't happen it throws a wrench into their circuitry—most of the time."

"Listen!" Nellie interrupted.

One of the guards was talking on a two-way radio outside the door, but he must have had an earphone in because they could only hear his side of the conversation.

"Yes, sir . . . no . . . We have two in custody. . . . Nellie and the Holt girl . . . If that's how you want to handle it . . . Let me look at a map. . . . I know the location. We'll be there in a few minutes."

The truck rumbled to life. They were on the move.

Phoenix had no idea how he had gotten to the front of the line, but it was too late to change positions now. The slippery steep path down to the river was only wide enough for one person. Alistair was about twenty feet behind him, holding on to roots sticking out from the dirt bank to keep himself steady. Fiske was next, followed by Ted and Natalie. Of all of them, Ted seemed to be doing the best at negotiating the treacherous descent. Phoenix could only guess it was because he was used to moving carefully and feeling his way. He waited for Alistair to catch up.

"Are you okay?"

"I'm fine," Alistair answered through clenched teeth. He was normally as neat as a pin, even in captivity, but his coverall was now soaked through with sweat and spattered with dirt. "I just have to move slowly, and I can't look down. I'm a little acrophobic."

Phoenix risked a glance at the boiling river a hundred feet below and his stomach lurched. He grabbed on to one of the roots, wondering if he suffered from fear of heights, too.

Or maybe it's the fact that I can't swim. Not that anyone could swim in those rapids.

"How's your hand?" Alistair asked, pushing on despite his obvious pain.

"It's okay," Phoenix said, which wasn't true. It was swollen, painful, and useless. He could only use his left hand to anchor himself in place and his heart squeezed each time he had to let go and take another step.

"Any sign of Reagan and Nellie?" Alistair asked the group behind him.

"No," a weary-looking Natalie replied.

Phoenix was about to volunteer to go look for them when the ground lurched beneath him. The wet dirt he was standing on seemed to quiver, then peel away from the path. Phoenix lunged for the side of the cliff, but his legs windmilled under him. It was too late. His world shifted into terrifying slow motion as he began to plunge into the rapids far below.

"Nooo!" Alistair leaped forward, falling hard on his bad knee, but all he could grab was Phoenix's injured hand.

Phoenix could hear the others screaming, but he couldn't see them. He was dangling over the river with the gray face of Alistair Oh looming above him. He frantically scrambled for a foothold, or something to grab on to with his good hand. But there was nothing beneath him but air. The pain from his injured hand was excruciating, and the blood made it slippery. He could feel Alistair's grip starting to fail.

"Hang on!" Alistair shouted. "I have you!"

Phoenix's weight was pulling Alistair closer and closer to the edge. Phoenix's eyes blurred with tears as the hideous truth struck him. If he didn't let go, they would both die.

Alistair must have seen the resolve in Phoenix's expression. "Don't let go!" Alistair pleaded.

Phoenix shook his head then, closing his eyes as tightly as he could. He pictured his mom's face, the good-night smile she gave him when she used to tuck him in.

And Phoenix let go.

CHAPTER 18

"Did someone just fall?"

Natalie barely heard the question over her sobs. Incredulous, she turned her head to see a hiker standing behind her.

"Did someone fall?" he repeated urgently.

Natalie looked at him in confusion. He was in his early twenties, carrying a backpack slung over his shoulder.

"Our friend just . . ." She choked up again. "He . . ."

"Stay exactly where you are," the man said. "I'm going to squeeze by you."

Before she could object, he slipped nimbly by her and Ted, who was frozen in horror.

Fiske stared at the man in disbelief. "Who are you? How did you—"

"Never mind that," the man interrupted. "The ground isn't stable!"

Together Fiske and the hiker pulled the devastated Alistair to his feet.

"I . . . I couldn't hold on. . . ."

"It's a long fall," the man said, looking over the edge. "But there's a chance he's still alive. Can he swim?"

"I don't know," Fiske said, looking with a spark of hope at Ted and Natalie.

Natalie shook her head. She didn't know, either.

"The rapids are bad through here," the man said. "But they flatten out about a mile downriver."

"Who are you?" Fiske asked.

"My name is Martin Holds. I was up on top when I heard someone yell."

"You got down here pretty quickly," Fiske said.

"I guess I did," Martin said. "I've been down this path before and I'm a mountain climber."

"Where are we?"

Martin looked confused. "You don't know?"

Fiske shook his head.

"Baden-Württemberg."

"Germany?" Fiske asked.

Martin nodded. "The Black Forest." He looked at their clothes and a whisper of alarm crossed his face.

"How can we get down there?"

"The trail's out. The only way around is to go back on top. I have a cell phone at camp. We can call for help." He gave Alistair a sympathetic look. "If your friend survived the fall, we'll find him."

Fiske shook his head. He could not believe that Phoenix was gone.

Natalie was the first to reach the top of the trail, but she'd barely stepped to safety when a hand grabbed her, covered her mouth, and threw her to the ground. Ted was next. Fiske tried to fight the guards off, but got a smack with a rifle butt for his trouble. With his bad knee, Alistair was subdued easily. Martin Holds was last. He was able to bloody a guard's nose and smash a fist into another guard's belly before he, too, was overwhelmed.

"Saved us from coming down to get you," the head guard said, looking down at the flex-cuffed prisoners. "Nice of you to come back up the trail."

Fiske was too exhausted and grief-stricken to respond, but Martin Holds struggled to turn over. "What's all this about?" he demanded.

The guard ignored him. "Where's the boy?"

"He fell," Fiske said.

"We'll see." He waved two guards down the trail. "Get up!"

When they didn't comply, the guards yanked them roughly to their feet.

"Get your hands off me!" Martin shouted.

"He has nothing to do with this!" Fiske insisted, breaking away to force himself between the guard and Martin. "He doesn't know anything. He was just trying to help us!"

"Wrong place at the wrong time," the head guard said. He took his pistol out of its holster and chambered a round.

"What do you think you're doing?" Martin shouted, his face stark with shock.

"Take them to the trucks," the head guard ordered, jerking his head toward the hostages.

"You can't do this!" Fiske yelled as they pushed him and the others into the woods. "He didn't do anything!"

A gunshot rang out behind them.

Natalie, Fiske, Ted, and Alistair each felt it in their guts.

Phoenix Wizard was too scared to scream as he fell. And he didn't have the time. The hundred-foot fall took only two seconds, but he hit the ice-cold water faster than his mom's car at top speed. He slammed down through the water and felt his legs crunch against the rocks at the bottom. The impact knocked the air out of him and he sucked in the frigid water. The current caught him immediately, scraping him over rocks and sucking him through whirlpools. When his lungs felt like they were about to burst, the current popped him out long enough to catch a frantic breath.

He knew his body couldn't take much more. His muscles had gone limp, and he barely had the strength to keep his hands up to protect his head from the jagged rocks that lined the banks and loomed up out of the water. Just as his battered body and brain were about to give up, he saw a long hanging branch. It was his only chance.

If I catch it, I live. If I miss it, I die.

He lunged for the branch, but his hand started to

slip. Gritting his teeth, he lunged a second time and let out a primal scream. This time his grip held and slowly, hand over hand, his shrapnel wound burning, he managed to pull himself onto shore. He lay there gasping for breath.

When Phoenix had enough strength to sit up, he assessed his situation. He guessed he must be at least a mile downstream by now. The others wouldn't have been able to make it past where the path collapsed. They'd have to double back and find another way down to the river — if they thought he survived. Phoenix fought the urge to rush back upstream as fast as possible and search for the others. His best option was to follow the river downstream and find help for himself and his friends.

He got shakily to his feet and tried to get his bearings. For as far as he could see in every direction were giant trees, steep hills, and snowcapped mountains.

How far is it to the nearest town? What if there isn't a road downriver?

The vastness of his surroundings seemed to shake right through him. Phoenix was alone in the wilderness.

CHAPTER 19

On the flight between Berlin and Timbuktu, Dan and Atticus used the private jet's restroom a record twenty-seven times each. Their room-service gorge from the night before had taken its toll on both of them. In between urgent trips down the aisle, they played video games on Jonah's sixty-inch high-definition monitor.

Amy and Jake were sitting as far away from the boys as they could. They both said that they wanted to sleep the whole way to Timbuktu, but the fifty-four times Dan or Atticus walked by, the two teenagers had their heads together talking, totally oblivious to everything around them.

Atticus returned from the restroom, sat down next to Dan, and blinked. "I think Jake has . . . It's almost too gross to think about. I think he likes Amy."

"Yeah?" Dan stared at the monitor. He was very close to achieving the next level. "By the way, you died when you were on the toilet. I tried to save you, but it was hard to use two controllers at once."

"What about Jake and Amy?" Atticus asked, craning his neck to get another look at his brother.

Dan scrunched up his face as if he were confronting a plate of lima beans. "If Jake likes her, he's in for a big disappointment. She only has eyes for Evan. When they're together, they're all 'You're so great; no, *you're* so great.' If you saw it, you'd gag. Speaking of which, I'm finally getting hungry again. How about you?"

Atticus reached up and punched the flight-attendant button.

"Desertification," Amy said as they stepped out onto the baking tarmac.

"I hear you," Dan said, holding his stomach. "I'm not going to eat another dessert for a week."

Atticus rolled his eyes. "She's not talking about *dessert*! She's talking about how the *desert* is reclaiming Timbuktu."

Dan had to admit it, it was difficult to distinguish the single-story airport buildings from the sand around them. The air seemed to crackle with heat. Battered airplanes were scattered haphazardly along the cracked runway, as if they had landed decades before and had never taken off again.

"It looks like the end of the world," Amy said.

"Well, it's sure *deserted*," Dan said. "Where is everybody?"

The only thing moving on the tarmac was blowing sand. The only thing moving inside the terminal was an old custodian sucking sand off the carpet with an ancient vacuum cleaner.

Atticus inched closer to his brother. "This is kind of creepy," he said.

"Yeah," Dan agreed. "It kind of reminds me of that end-of-the-world game we were playing on the airplane."

"Without the zombies," Atticus said, frowning suspiciously at the landscape around them.

"I'm glad to see you both utilized your time so well on the plane," Amy said.

"Yeah? What did you and Jake do?" Dan shot back.

Amy lifted her chin. "We learned that Timbuktu was once a safe haven for scholars and the intellectual hub for most of Islam."

"There's no reference to an 'Apology for a Great Transgression' anywhere on the web," Jake said. "But Timbuktu has a half a dozen libraries, with thousands of ancient manuscripts, most of which are uncataloged. Whatever Vesper One's looking for, it's probably in one of those libraries."

"How many thousands?" Atticus asked, a spark of interest showing behind his glasses.

"Mark this down," Jake said. "There's something my brother doesn't know."

"Seven hundred thousand," Amy said quietly. The vast number silenced them all for a moment.

"That's only one hundred seventy-five thousand each." Atticus cocked his head doubtfully.

No one responded.

Dan looked at his watch. "We have twenty hours left, so we better get started."

Amy opened the door marked *Passenger Pick-Up* in French.

There was only one taxi. The driver was lying on the hood asleep, but he sat up and stretched as they approached. He gave his brown and gray beard a good scratch, took a sip of water, swished it around, then spit it out on the sand-covered asphalt.

"My name is Bart. I am at your service."

"Is your name really Bart?" Atticus asked.

The man raised an eyebrow. "If you prefer you can call me Basharat Antarah Rawahah Tajamul."

"Bart works for me," Dan said.

"Your English is excellent," Jake said. "Elijah told me it would be."

Amy stared at him. "Who?"

"Elijah Smith," Jake explained. "My dad's travel agent. I texted him and asked if he knew anyone in Timbuktu that could show us around. He said we could trust Mr. Tajamul with our lives."

Amy gritted her teeth. "You could have mentioned this to me," she said.

Jake smiled and shrugged, which irritated her even more.

Bart looked at Amy. "My French is even better than

my English. My father sent me to private school in Paris and the University of California at Berkeley. He wanted me to better myself. But as you can see . . ." He gestured to his tattered clothes and dented taxi.

"I'm not sure we'll need your services after all," Amy said.

Jake frowned. "We'll at least need a ride into town."

"How much?" Amy asked Bart.

"Seventy-five thousand CFA," Bart said.

"And how much is that in dollars?"

"One hundred and fifty."

"Outrageous," Amy said, snapping her eyes over at Jake. He looked a little surprised, too, which gave her some satisfaction.

"For two hundred dollars I could be at your disposal for the next twenty-four hours. Or perhaps you already know your way around Timbuktu?"

Amy pulled Dan to the side. She trusted his instincts. "What do you think?" she whispered.

"He seems okay," Dan answered. "If he was a Vesper he wouldn't be asking for that much, because he wouldn't want to lose the job. And we are in a hurry."

Amy nodded and turned back to Bart.

"All right," she said. "Half now. Half when we leave."

Bart gave her a slight bow. "It is a deal."

Amy counted out the money.

Milos Vanek was at an airport four thousand miles away. Unlike the Timbuktu airport, Mumbai International was teeming with thousands of people in bright clothes hauling impossibly huge loads of luggage and packages. He wove his way through the throng as he spoke to a colleague at the Mumbai Interpol headquarters.

It appeared that Dan Cahill had been telling the truth. Jonah Wizard had been spotted in Mumbai earlier that day. A video of the famous entertainer dancing with a charmed cobra had gone viral, and now every young person in Mumbai was out with their camera phone looking for him.

Vanek would be looking for him, too.

CHAPTER 20

Nellie had been sobbing for more than an hour straight, her injuries all but forgotten in her grief over Phoenix. The thoughts of what she should have done pummeled her. She should never have stayed behind with Reagan. She should have kept everyone together. The others assured her that it would have made no difference, but she didn't believe them. He was just a little kid, and he'd trusted her. She wiped the tears away with the back of her hand and took a deep breath. There were other little kids in the truck, and they needed her just as much as he had.

Get it together, Gomez. Focus on those who are still here.

"I can't believe they shot Martin Holds," Fiske said.

They had told her and Reagan about the hiker and his sudden murder.

If the Vespers could murder a completely innocent bystander, what do they have in mind for us?

The hostages had been in the back of the panel truck for hours without water, food, or relief. No amount of pounding, kicking, yelling, or pleading would get the guards to open the door. Reagan had suggested they rock the truck until they tipped it over.

"Why?" Natalie snapped. "So they can drag us out and stuff us into another?"

"How about just to annoy them?" Reagan offered.

Nellie managed to smile despite her grief.

"We're being punished," Fiske said. "As soon as we are softened up, they'll put us back into the bunker."

But Fiske was wrong. The truck started to move, speeding up, slowing down, bouncing them around like rocks in a tin can. Finally, hours later, it shuddered to a halt.

The door swung open.

"Get out!" yelled a massive man with a thick black beard.

Nellie climbed out, covering her eyes against the fading sunlight. By the look of it, they were still in the Black Forest. She hoped they wouldn't have to hike. Alistair was barely able to stand on his own.

"We need a doctor!" Nellie said.

"If you don't shut up, you'll need a mortician," a guard said. "Now move!" He pointed his rifle at a steep trail leading off into the woods.

There were twice as many guards as there had been at the other location. Some were on four-wheelers, some were on foot. All of them were heavily armed. Nellie took Ted's hand.

"They're not wearing balaclavas," Reagan whispered to Nellie as they started up the trail.

Nellie was worried about that, too. The masks had been intimidating, but the lack of masks was foreboding. It meant the Vespers no longer cared if they were recognized.

They have no intention of letting us go.

She scanned the area for a way to escape. If one of them got away, maybe they could bring back help.

"We'll get our chance," Reagan whispered, as if she were reading Nellie's mind. "Right now we need to act defeated. Let them think they've broken us."

"I am broken," Nellie said. The bites on her leg and face throbbed.

"Wounded, not broken," Ted said.

"Maybe," Nellie said, "but I'm not so sure about Alistair."

He could barely walk, and hadn't said a word in over an hour. He'd fallen on a sharp rock when he lunged to catch Phoenix, taking a deep puncture to his bad knee. But Phoenix's fall had hurt him much worse than the leg injury.

They trudged on for about a half a mile, until Nellie got fed up.

"That's it!" she said, sitting down in the middle of the trail.

"Get up," the guard with the black beard said.

She shook her head. "Nope." He pointed his rifle at her, but Nellie stared back at him.

"You think I won't?" he responded.

"I don't care." She crossed her arms and continued her defiant stare.

"Look," the guard said, faltering. "It's not that much farther."

"One of us can barely walk. One of us is blind." Nellie said. "Put them on the four-wheelers and I'll get up."

"Forget it."

"Fine." Nellie pointed at her forehead. "Squeeze the trigger."

The guard slowly raised his rifle, but Nellie met his gaze straight on. She didn't even blink.

The guard swore, lowered his rifle, and walked back down the trail. A couple minutes later, he came back on a four-wheeler, a second one rumbling up behind him. He pointed at Ted and Alistair. "You two climb on back. If you try anything funny I *will* shoot her." He looked at Nellie. "Anything else?"

"Water," Nellie said promptly.

"You're pushing your luck."

"If I'm given a choice between dying of thirst or a bullet, I'll take the bullet."

Black Beard glared at her for a second, then reached around into a side pack for six bottles of water. He got off the four-wheeler and then tossed the bottles to them one at a time, saving Ted for last. He smiled, and tossed Ted's bottle rather hard.

Ted caught it with one hand. "Thanks."

"I thought you were blind," the astonished guard said.

"Just my eyes. My ears work fine. I heard it coming."

"Freak," the guard muttered.

An hour later they reached the end of the trail. Stretching through the woods for as far as they could see in both directions was a twelve-foot-high electrified fence topped by razor wire.

"What is this place?" Fiske asked.

The guards waved them through a steel gate without answering. On the other side of the fence was a gigantic compound. In the center of it was a white geodesic dome.

"Describe it for me," Ted said.

"We're in a clearing on top of a mountain," Fiske said.

"Roughly the size of four football fields," Reagan added.

"There's a white dome in the middle," Natalie said. "It looks kind of like a high-end igloo."

"It would be almost impossible to get all this up here without a road," Alistair said.

The group turned toward him in surprise. It was the first complete sentence he had uttered in hours.

At that moment, an airship carrying a cargo net with an immense load of crates appeared over the tops of the trees.

Nellie pointed at the sky. "Airship," she said.

"Get moving!" a guard shouted.

They pushed and prodded the hostages through the dome entrance.

There were dozens of men and women inside, each one hard at work moving equipment around on forklifts, consulting digital pads, or talking on flashing Bluetooths. Alistair looked around in awe. "They're building something. It's . . ." He paused. "What *is* this?"

But the guards didn't give them time for a closer look. They hustled the hostages toward an elevator.

"Get in."

The group shuffled inside.

"Photo op," one of the guards said. He videotaped them for a few seconds, then nodded. The door slid closed and they shot up several floors.

They expected another set of guards to be waiting for them. Instead, the doors opened directly into a twenty-by-twenty-foot room. Directly in front of them was a floor-to-ceiling mirror. They watched themselves step out of the elevator.

"I assume that's a two-way mirror," Fiske said.

Along the left and right walls were eight cots bolted to the wall, end to end, four to a side. In the right-hand corner was a stainless steel sink and toilet.

Nellie walked closer to the mirror. One side of her face had puffed up so the skin was as tight as a balloon. She traced the ring of angry red bite marks from her hairline to halfway across her cheek.

"There's food." Alistair said. "Bottled water." He

was pulling out boxes from under the cots. The others rushed over to help.

"M-R-E's?" Reagan read out the initials.

"Meals Ready to Eat. United States military meals."

"Martin Holds said we were in the Black Forest," Fiske said.

Everyone looked at each other in confusion.

Reagan was the first to pull open her meal. The others followed, tearing open the packets. Ted was the only one who didn't move.

"Here," Natalie said, "I'll open an MRE for you."

"Thanks," Ted said. "But it's not that. Maybe we should . . . I don't know. Maybe we should have a moment of silence for Phoenix?"

Everyone stopped eating.

"That's an excellent idea," Fiske said.

They closed their eyes and bowed their heads.

Phoenix was having his own MRE. He wasn't sure what it was, but he guessed it was a trout. It had taken him an hour to scoop it out of a shallow pool and onto the riverbank. He was exhausted and wet. He'd already seen two bears and heard what he thought was a mountain lion. He didn't know Germany had mountain lions. The bears had ignored him, but not the sharp rocks, thorns, and branches. He had scrapes and bruises from the top of his head to his feet.

But I'm alive.

At first he had made his way downriver slowly, hoping that the others would catch up with him. When there was no sign of them, he'd started to pick up his pace, hoping to find a road or a house. So far there had been nothing but untouched wilderness. Still, the river had to lead somewhere, if nowhere else than to the ocean. If he got to the sea he could follow the shoreline to a town.

But to get there, I have to survive.

He hit the fish in the head with a rock and waited for it to stop flopping before he took a bite.

Sushi.

Bart screeched the taxi to a stop in front of the Ahmed Baba Institute, creating a choking cloud of red dust and blue exhaust, which the people loitering outside the institute completely ignored. The library was two stories tall and relatively new. It looked like it had been dropped out of the sky into the sandlot between two very old buildings.

"There are eighteen thousand ancient manuscripts inside, give or take," Bart said.

"Ahmed Baba was Timbuktu's most famous scholar. Some believe he was a Mujaddid, a very religious man," Jake said.

Dan looked down at his phone. "On a different subject, do any of you have a cell signal?"

They all looked at their phones and shook their heads.

"Reception is very spotty in Timbuktu," Bart said. "But we all have cell phones in case a signal blows in with the sand. You will know when you have bars. Everyone will rush into the area hoping to take advantage. A moment later the signal will move down the street. It is like the wind."

They had decided to split into two teams in order to cover more libraries and museums. Amy and Jake would start on one end of the city and Dan and Atticus on the other end, working their way toward each other.

"How will we stay in touch?" Jake said. "Maybe we should stay together."

"Except for the fact that you and Atticus are the only two that can read the Arabic manuscripts," Dan said. "I can't even read the name on this building. It looks like a bunch of snakes."

"Dan's right," Amy said. "We don't have time to do it any other way."

"I have an idea," Bart said. "I can watch the boys for one hundred more dollars."

They had almost forgotten that he was in the front seat.

"Fifty," Amy said.

"Seventy-five."

"Sixty."

"Done."

"Hey!" Dan said. "I don't need a babysitter!" Atticus nodded in vigorous agreement.

Amy ignored him. "How will we contact you?"

"We will hire a boy," Bart answered. "A runner. I know just the one. We call him La Souris, or the Mouse. Timbuktu is small. You can get from one end to the other in less than two hours walking."

Then why did we hire you? Dan thought, glaring at the back of Bart's head.

Bart got out of the taxi and gestured at someone hanging outside the institute, who in turn went to someone else and so on. Two minutes later a little boy who looked only about five years old came running down the street. He was wearing ragged shorts and a worn Jonah Wizard T-shirt that read: *Wiz up?* On his feet were an expensive-looking pair of running shoes — a couple of sizes too big. The haggling over his fee took twice as long as it did for the Mouse to get there. They finally settled on twenty-five dollars and a Jonah Wizard souvenir pen and pencil set, which Dan had taken from Jonah's private jet.

Amy and Jake got out of the taxi and watched it drive away.

"I'm not comfortable with this," Jake said.

"You hired him," Amy shot back.

"I should have told you . . . sorry."

Amy peeped over at him. She wondered how she could be so mad at Jake one moment, and completely forgive him the next. "Apology accepted," she said.

"It's just that I have a bad feeling about this."

"Welcome to the Cahill family," Amy said, striding into the institute. "You'll get used to it."

There weren't many cars on the narrow, sandblown streets, but there were a lot of camels, goats, donkeys, and people, which slowed the taxi to a honking crawl.

"It's like we've traveled back to biblical times," Atticus said, his face glued to the window.

Dan was not nearly as excited. Timbuktu was the most impoverished city he had ever been in. Garbage blew down the narrow streets, and there were beggars on every corner. It was hard to believe that the city was once the intellectual capital of Africa. It was so depressing that he wondered why people lived here, or if they had a choice.

"What do people do here for a living?" he asked Bart.

"They get by," he answered.

"Why do you stay here?" Atticus asked.

"Because it's my home." He pointed out a two-story building. "That's the Grand Marché. Timbuktu's biggest market. If you get a chance, you'll want to go through the stalls and buy some souvenirs."

"We won't have much time for shopping," Dan said.

"You should at least go up to the roof. It offers the best view of the Sahara in the city. I could pull over and you could run up to the top."

"No time," Dan said.

Bart shot him a curious glance. "What exactly is it that you're looking for in such a hurry?"

Dan and Atticus caught each other's eyes. "We're just curious about the Timbuktu manuscripts," Dan answered. "But our parents would only give us twenty-four hours to look at them before we have to return to school."

"So your parents are very strict," Bart said with a smile. "They would only loan you their private jet for a day."

"Something like that."

Bart the babysitter is way too nosy.

Bart pulled up to a building and stopped. "This is the Mamma Haidara Library." He turned and looked at them. "The Haidaras are old Timbuktu. The collection has been in their family for hundreds of years. They are going to be very suspicious of two American boys asking to see their manuscripts."

The library was not nearly as nice as the Ahmed Baba Institute. It was surrounded by a six-foot-high wall made of yellow bricks, and the entrance was through an intimidating metal gate painted black.

"Do you know the mom?" Dan asked.

Bart laughed. "*Mamma* does not refer to a mom. It is like a first name. But to answer your question, yes, I know the Haidaras."

Atticus brightened. "Maybe you can come in and give us an introduction!"

"That would not be wise. I was once married to a Haidara girl. It did not work out. There are ill feelings between our families. In fact, it would be best not to say who drove you here if the subject comes up. I will park around the corner."

Atticus and Dan climbed out of the back and watched Bart drive away.

"Perfect," Dan said.

"What do you mean, perfect?" Atticus said. "It would have been a lot better for us if Bart and the Haidaras were best friends."

"I meant it's perfect he's parking around the corner. We're going to have to ditch our babysitter."

"Why?"

"Because he's asking too many questions that we can't answer. As soon as we get done here, we'll head to the next library on foot . . . Bartless."

Jake and Amy couldn't get over the number of manuscripts at the Ahmed Baba Institute. The curator, Mr. Bazzi, could not have been more helpful or friendly. He swept them through the huge collection with great pride. But seeing row upon row of floor-to-ceiling cases was discouraging. This was just the first library. How were they ever going to find the "Apology" in this haystack of ancient texts?

"Of course, these are just the manuscripts that we have cataloged and digitized," Bazzi explained.

"You have them on hard disk?" Amy was encouraged.

"A portion of them, yes."

"Are they searchable?" Jake asked.

"Of course. But before I direct you to a computer, allow me to show you one of our more notable finds."

Amy was desperate to check out the computer, but she and Jake smiled politely and followed. Bazzi's cooperation was too valuable to risk offending him.

He led them to a glass case with an open manuscript inside. "What do you see?"

Jake leaned forward to examine the pages. "A diagram of the planets radiating out from the sun."

"Exactly! Just as Copernicus proposed in his *On the Revolutions of the Celestial Spheres* in 1543."

"Interesting," Amy said, glancing around for the computer, eager to end the tour and get to work.

Bazzi smiled. "I think you do not understand," he said. "This manuscript was written by one of our Timbuktu scholars two hundred years before Copernicus was born!"

"Wow!" Jake said. "That *is* amazing!" He peered down at the manuscript. "What's all the writing in the margins? It's so small it's hard to read."

Amy looked impatiently at her watch, but Bazzi and Jake didn't seem to notice.

"Ah, yes," Bazzi said. "It is doodling, as you might say in your country. Back when the scholars were here, paper was worth more than gold. They had to use any blank paper they could find, even if it was another scholar's manuscript."

"What kind of doodling?"

"Diary entries, scientific theories, to-do lists, maps, poetry—"

"That's all fascinating," Amy said, making sure they both saw her look at her watch this time. "But I'm afraid we're on a tight schedule."

"Of course." Bazzi gave her an apologetic nod. "I do

get carried away. Not many outside people come to the institute to talk about the manuscripts."

Jake nudged Amy's side. "Just a couple more questions," he said.

Amy could have killed him.

"Have you ever come across any manuscripts written in Latin?" she asked, thinking back to Vesper One's text. Perhaps that would help them narrow their search.

"No. But as you probably know, Arabic is considered the Latin of Africa. And Timbuktu was the center of learning. At its peak, there were twenty-five thousand scholars and students in the city, sharing information in much the same way information is now shared on the Internet. Millions of documents were created here during that time."

"What happened?" Amy asked, curious despite herself.

"Invasion," Bazzi answered. "The manuscripts were hidden in the walls of houses, in dry wells, buried in the sands of the Sahara so the invaders could not destroy them. The manuscripts were preserved by the dry air for hundreds of years. It wasn't until quite recently that people felt secure enough to start bringing them to light. Last week, five hundred manuscripts were brought in. The week before, twice that many. It is one of the biggest collections of ancient manuscripts in the world, but because of our isolation few people know about them."

"Who brings them in?" Jake asked.

"Old Timbuktu families, the military, desert tribes. We pay them what we can for retrieving our heritage, but funding is limited."

Amy looked around at the thick walls that housed thousands of manuscripts. It was as if rivers of ancient knowledge converged within the institute, safe for another century. "We'll make a donation before we leave," Amy said.

"That's very kind of you. We will accept it, but you can do something else for us."

"Sure," Amy said.

"Most people know about the famous cathedrals of Europe, or the caravan routes in the East," Bazzi said. "But few people know about the ancient route where knowledge was shared. We call it the Ink Road, and you are at its epicenter." He pointed at the manuscript in the glass case. "Who's to say? Perhaps there is something in one of the manuscripts that has yet to be discovered by modern man. Will you tell people about our manuscripts? The only way to preserve them is for people to know."

"We'll tell everyone," she promised, and mentally wrote out a check that would ensure the institute was funded for another fifty years. It wasn't always awful to be a Cahill.

"Thank you," Bazzi said. "Now, if you will follow me, our best computer is in our cataloging room."

He led them through a maze of glass cases to a small

door in the back. When he opened it, a blast of stale air hit them.

"Preservatives," Bazzi explained. "Perhaps a little mold. You will get used to the odor." He switched on the lights and then headed back to his desk.

It wasn't a room. It was a warehouse. Manuscripts were stacked on racks twenty feet high.

Amy went pale. "It looks like an ancient recycling center. We'll never find the 'Apology' here."

"It's not as hopeless as you think," Jake said. "Remember the margin of error."

"What are you talking about?"

"Vesper's note," Jake said. " 'Off to Timbuktu you go. No margin for error.'"

Amy was still confused.

Jake picked up a manuscript from one of the shelves and pointed to the doodlings around the primary text. "I'm guessing the 'Apology' is written in the *margin* of one of the manuscripts, in Latin."

"That has to be it!" Amy threw her arms around him. Jake pulled her tightly to him . . . until they both realized what he was doing. The two snapped apart as if they had been shocked, but their eyes met again. Amy's face was flaming and even Jake looked a little flushed. They tilted closer and closer together, as if some magnetic force was pulling at them. Jake leaned and Amy leaned, the space between them growing smaller and smaller. And then their lips touched.

Amy jumped back like a scalded cat, leaping

away from an equally flustered Jake Rosenbloom.

"I'm—um—" Amy hadn't been tongue-tied like this in weeks. She took a deep breath, but it caught in her throat and her voice came out as a squeak. "I'll go out and Mouse the Dan." Her cheeks burned. "Tell the Mouse to find Dan! I'll go out." She turned around and marched resolutely to the door.

"Yeah . . . uh . . ." Jake's mouth wasn't cooperating, either. "Good idea. I'll . . . uh . . . I'll start skimming the margins."

But he was speaking to an empty room. Amy Cahill was gone.

CHAPTER 22

As Bart predicted, Dan and Atticus were not welcomed with open arms at Mamma Haidara's. The librarian, a Mr. Srour, nearly tossed them out as soon as they walked in. He was an older man with white hair, wearing stained khaki pants, a white shirt, and a tattered sports coat. Atticus pulled out his Harvard student card, but Srour scowled at it through thick glasses as if it were fake. Atticus's next tactic was to drop a name. "Perhaps you've heard of my father," Atticus said. "His name is Dr. Mark Rosenbloom."

"The archaeologist?"

Atticus nodded.

"I met him," Srour admitted grudgingly. "Several years ago."

"That's right!" Atticus said. "I'd forgotten. He was here to examine an old dig outside the city near the Niger River."

Dan interrupted. "Dr. Rosenbloom sent us here to find something called the 'Apology for a Great Transgression.'"

"Ahhh," Srour said.

"You know it?" Dan asked, excitedly.

"No," Srour said, shaking his head. "There are hundreds of thousands of manuscripts scattered throughout the city in libraries like ours, in museums, and in private homes," Srour said. "I've done the calculations. It would take one hundred scholars twenty years to read them all, and that's if they each read one full manuscript every day."

"We don't have that much time!" Dan said.

"All I can do is look up the phrase on my computer and see if it is in our database. If you'll wait here." He walked through a doorway in back of the reception area.

"There aren't a hundred of *us*," Dan said, "and we don't have twenty years to skim a million moldering manuscripts. We have less than twenty hours, or someone is going to die."

The boys immediately split up and started sorting through the manuscripts on display.

After a few minutes, Srour came back through the door, shaking his head. "I did the search several ways. The word *apology* doesn't appear at all, and our collection is completely digitized. I'd recommend examining the other collections. There's a map of them on the wall in my office."

They followed him into his office. The map took up most of the wall behind his desk. It was dotted by red and blue pins. "The blue pins are the public collections," Srour explained. "The red pins are the private collections. The private collections are in people's homes. We are trying to convince them to bring the manuscripts in, but people are reluctant to give up their family heirlooms."

There were a lot more red pins than blue. And there were a lot more places holding manuscripts than Atticus would have guessed. Dan was staring at the map as if he were hypnotized by it.

"I guess we better get going. Thanks for your time."

"I'm sorry I wasn't more help," Srour said.

Out on the street, Atticus asked Dan what the plan was.

"The plan is in serious jeopardy," Dan said. "According to Srour's map, almost every other building in Timbuktu has a load of ancient manuscripts. To find them all we'd have to almost do a house-to-house search. I guess we should start with the blue pins. When we get done with those, we'll start in on the red pins."

Dan's head was reeling. Vesper One's ransom demands were always difficult, but this one was like looking for a needle in a haystack. Like a needle in a thousand haystacks. His chest tightened. He could almost feel the time counting down with each heartbeat.

"What about Bart?" asked Atticus.

"We sure don't need a taxi." Dan pointed to a building less than half a block away. "That's the next blue pin, and there are two reds in between."

The Mouse ran up to them and started jabbering in a combination of Arabic and French. When the Mouse paused for breath, Atticus turned to Dan and translated.

"He says that Jake and Amy think the apology will be written in the margins, not the main text."

"Of course," Dan said. "'Margin of error'! Tell him about the blue and red pins. Even with the margins, it's still going to be impossible to flip through all the manuscripts. Someone's going to have to get lucky."

Dan told the Mouse about the blue and red pens. The small boy nodded, then sprinted back down the sandy street, dodging camels, goats, and . . .

"What are people from Timbuktu called?" Dan asked.

Atticus wasn't sure. "Timbuktians?" he guessed.

"Let's go meet some of them."

CHAPTER 23

Amy walked back into the library warehouse after getting the message from the Mouse. Jake was busy skimming manuscripts for Latin. She wanted to talk to him about the . . . thing. The thing that had sort of happened between them. The thing that was never going to happen again. But the blue and red pins were a lot more important at the moment.

"Wow," Jake said, looking everywhere but at her. "That many?"

"Dan has perfect recall."

Jake gazed at the shelves of manuscripts they hadn't gotten to. "Then we have a problem."

Amy nodded. "That's why I was thinking we should split up."

Jake jerked his head toward her, alarm written all over his face.

"I didn't mean—" Amy stopped herself. She didn't know what she meant. "I'll go to the next library while you finish here."

"Stay here!" Jake blurted. "I mean, we could finish

in half the time if we work together. It's the same difference either way."

Amy shook her head and let her hair cover her flaming cheeks. "We have to streamline the process. I can do a computer search at the next library while you finish up here."

"I don't think it's safe for you to be running around on your own."

Now Amy had to smile. The only reason she and Dan hadn't been kidnapped like the others was because she had single-handedly punched and kicked their three assailants into submission. Well, she had to admit that Dan had helped by dousing the three men with gasoline and threatening to light them on fire. But still.

"I appreciate your concern," she said. And she meant it. "I'll take the Mouse with me. He'll come and get you if there's even a hint of a problem."

"Fine," Jake said, but she could tell he was unhappy. "I'll come and get you as soon as I'm done here."

The first three places Dan and Atticus went into were complete busts. None of them had heard of the "Apology for a Great Transgression" and all their manuscripts had been digitized. They walked down the street toward the fourth collection and were stopped in their tracks by a noxious smell and a swarm of flies.

"Butcher shop," Atticus said.

"Camel heads," Dan said.

There were six of them stacked in a short pyramid outside the butcher's door.

"The sign says the camel heads are eight dollars apiece," Atticus said.

"What a bargain!" Dan said. He took his camera phone out to get a photo of the grisly sight. "Remind me not to order any red meat while we're here."

As he snapped the picture, his phone chimed.

"I've got bars!"

He wasn't the only one. People poured out of the shops and houses, whipping cell phones out of their pockets and robes. Dan and Atticus were jostled, elbowed, and stepped on as the Timbuktians jockeyed for position to catch a signal. After a few seconds there was a collective moan of disgust as the elusive signal drifted elsewhere.

The crowd dispersed. Some returned to their homes and shops, others ran down the street holding their cell phones in the air to try to catch the tail end of the signal.

Someone shouted. Dan and Atticus turned from the signal catchers and saw a bloody-aproned butcher pointing angrily at the pyramid of camel heads. The top one was missing.

Looking at the pile of heads, something snapped in Dan's head.

Heads for Phoenix. Tails for Oh.

The camel heads didn't look nearly as funny as they had a second before.

He looked down at his screen.

```
I set you up to SUCCEED at the Pergamon
Museum. And succeed you did. I will tell
you all about The Book of Ingenious
Devices when I see you. I can't tell you
how much I am looking forward to that
day. AJT
```

"Succeeded for him," Dan said.

"What?" Atticus asked.

"None of your business." Dan stomped away. Atticus might be a genius, but there were things even he couldn't understand. He didn't know what it was like being a Cahill. To know that nothing was what it seemed. To have a painful past that refused to stay buried.

Timbuktu wasn't the only victim of desertification.

Dan was afraid he could feel his own soul turning to dust.

CHAPTER 24

Erasmus sat in the Starcity Cinema watching *Zindagi Na Milegi Dobara*, or *You Won't Get Life Again*. This was his third time seeing the comedy and he found it just as funny as the first time.

He grabbed a handful of popcorn from the bucket in his lap and wondered how many films he had seen in his life.

Hundreds. Maybe thousands. I should make a list.

When he was on the run with his mom, they went to the movies every day, no matter what city or country they were hiding in. The theaters were dark and safe, and the films took their minds off the fact that people were trying to kill them. Erasmus had honed his language skills in front of the big screen. He had wanted to grow up to be a film director. Then his mother was killed.

He felt tears fill his eyes. He could be a sap when he was watching a film he knew she would like.

His cell phone vibrated. He wiped his eyes with a greasy napkin, then slipped the phone out of his leather pocket.

```
The woman is preparing to leave. She has
requested a taxi.
```

The text was from a server at the restaurant inside
the Orchid Hotel.

Erasmus got up and quickly exited the theater. As
he made his way down the crowded street to his motorcycle, a second text arrived. It was from Hamilton.

```
We may have a problem.
```

Hamilton wasn't much for words, which Erasmus
liked, but he wished the boy had included a few more
to describe what the problem was. He got on his motorcycle and gunned it, making it to the hotel in less than
five minutes.

Hamilton was exactly where he had left him a few
hours earlier, but there was no sign of Jonah.

Across the street at the Orchid were two police cars
and a couple dozen young people brandishing camera
phones.

"Where's Jonah?" Erasmus asked, still straddling
his motorcycle.

"Yo, dude," a voice whispered behind him. "It wasn't
my fault!"

Erasmus turned his head. Jonah was peeking
around the corner of a rather noxious overflowing
dumpster. He had on fake glasses, a gaudy Hawaiian
shirt, baggy Bermuda shorts, black socks, and sandals.

Erasmus cracked a grin. "You might as well have put on a neon sign that says *I'm trying not to look like Jonah Wizard*."

"I think I might have made a mistake," Jonah said miserably.

"You danced with a cobra," Erasmus said.

"YouTube?"

Erasmus nodded.

"Sorry, dude."

"You lasted longer than I thought."

The police were clearing the crowd so a taxi could pull up to the entrance.

"Luna's on the move," Erasmus said. "That's her taxi. When she gets into it, we'll follow. Stay two car lengths behind me. There are more motorcycles than cars here so I don't think she'll notice us. But this could be a ruse of some kind. Luna might ride around in the taxi for a while and come right back here to see if anyone is tailing her." The hotel doors pushed open. "Here she comes."

The crowd didn't pay the slightest attention to the little old lady climbing into the back of the taxi. Erasmus pulled out into traffic behind it.

Hamilton jumped on the rickshaw motorcycle and kicked it to life. Jonah crouched down and hobbled toward the rickshaw so he couldn't be seen from across the street.

"Hurry up!" Hamilton yelled.

"Yo, dude, it's my turn to drive!"

"Just jump in back or I'll leave you behind."

Their argument turned heads across the street.

A young girl gasped, turned bright red, and started hopping up and down and pointing. "Jonah Wizard!" she screamed.

The rickshaw was not nearly as fast as Erasmus's motorcycle. Ham and Jonah wouldn't have caught up at all if it hadn't been for the snarled traffic on the freeway and Hamilton's crazy driving. Jonah bounced around in the back, keeping an eye out behind him for oncoming fans, and on the cars in front of him for oncoming death. He tore off his ridiculous disguise and struggled into one of Ham the Giant's tracksuits, which wasn't easy in the backseat of a rickshaw.

So far they'd ditched the fans, but Jonah knew from experience that this could change in a split second. The fans were on their cell phones, calling friends and tweeting. *Jonah Wizard is headed west on Nehru Road in a motorcycle rickshaw! He's being driven by a guy that looks like a marine wearing a powder blue tracksuit!*

It wouldn't be long before they were spotted by a driver or passenger. All it would take is one tweet, and the fans would converge from all directions like hungry locusts.

Hamilton was paying no attention to Jonah. He was focused intently on Erasmus weaving in and out of traffic in front of them. He had no idea which taxi Erasmus was even following — there were at least fifty on the road. After about a half an hour traffic started to thin out and Ham got a bead on the car they were tailing. Luna's taxi exited the freeway, turned south toward Mahim Bay, snaked its way through several side streets, and finally came to a stop in front of a three-story warehouse. Erasmus pulled into an alley a half a block away. Hamilton turned in behind him.

"Stay out of sight," Erasmus said. He crept up to the alley entrance and peeked around to look up the street. "She's in the building. The taxi left. We'll wait until it gets dark, then move in closer."

Erasmus turned around to the two boys. "I think Luna's led us to a Vesper safe house. It's the first time I've ever found one."

He took up a position at the end of the alley and watched the warehouse. Jonah and Hamilton sat in the rickshaw and watched him. An hour passed before Erasmus moved. For a big man he was very light on his feet.

"Dude moves like a puma," Jonah said to Ham as they followed.

"Keep your voices down!" Erasmus whispered.

He led them to a stack of pallets directly across from the warehouse where they could watch without being seen. The third-floor lights were on, but they couldn't spot anyone through the grimy windows.

"I thought Vespers were rich," Hamilton said. "You'd think they could do better than this dump."

"The building and location are exactly what I expected," Erasmus corrected. "It doesn't look like much, so no one thinks about it. I'd guess the lower floor is a legitimate business and the upper floors belong to the Vespers. The building's old. They might have been operating out of it for hundreds of years. Did you see Mahim Fort when we drove in?"

"I was too busy keeping up with you," Hamilton said.

"I was too busy trying to get my pants on," Jonah said.

"It's only a couple miles away. The fort was built in the fifteen hundreds. This warehouse is built out of the same stone."

"You know what's weird about this street?" Hamilton said.

Erasmus shook his head.

"No people."

"Dude's right," Jonah said.

Erasmus said nothing.

The light went out on the third floor.

"Do you see the flashlight?" Erasmus asked, pointing at one of the windows.

"Do you think the building has more than one exit?" Hamilton asked.

"If it's a Vesper stronghold, it will have a dozen exits."

They saw a flash of light on the second level, then the first. Luna Amato came out the front door, looked up and down the street, then set off briskly walking north.

"Follow her," Erasmus said. "See where she goes."

"What about you?" Hamilton asked.

Erasmus flashed his grin. "I'm going to do a little breaking and entering."

CHAPTER 25

As Amy made her way to the second library, her phone chimed. She wasn't the only one to hear it. Phones shot out of pockets all around her as people started chatting. She had a text from Erasmus.

```
Luna has led us to a Vesper stronghold.
Do you want me to go in and check it out?
```

She had only one bar and one second to decide.

```
Yes.
```

The messages swooshed into the ether a moment before the signal vanished. The people around her moaned and cursed in frustration.

She walked into the library. Before she could even say hello, the man behind the desk spoke. "Let me guess—the 'Apology for a Great Transgression.'"

"You've heard of it?"

"Not until an hour ago, when your friends came in here and asked about it."

"Friends?" Amy asked. Dan and Atticus were on the other side of town.

"Perhaps I am jumping to conclusions. If so, I apologize. There are not a lot of young Americans in Timbuktu. I just assumed that you were associated." The man's eyes flashed. "And they were not friendly."

"That doesn't sound like my group," Amy said. "What did they look like?"

"Blond. Blue-eyed. Twins—a man and a woman."

Amy's stomach dropped to her feet. "The Wyomings!"

The man shrugged. "They did not say where they were from."

She ran frantically through the scenarios. *Did they arrive before or after us? How many libraries have they been to?* But it was the last question that tortured her. *If they find the 'Apology' first, what happens to the hostages?*

"Did they tell you that the 'Apology' is in Latin?" she asked.

"Yes. Our collection is not nearly as extensive as Ahmed Baba's, but ninety-five percent has been digitized. I have not read every manuscript, but I have certainly skimmed them. I did not see Latin in any of the margins."

"I don't think I mentioned that I had been to the Ahmed Baba Institute," Amy said suspiciously, drawing herself up to her full height. "Or that I was looking for anything in the margin of the manuscripts."

"You did not," the man agreed. "But everybody in Timbuktu knows what you're after. Did you really think you could fly in on a private jet and not be noticed? Mr. Bazzi called me. And I'm sure he called others, just as I did. If the manuscript is in Timbuktu, it will be found." He laughed. "Mr. Bazzi has been waiting for your boyfriend to leave so he can search the warehouse himself."

"He's not my boyfriend," Amy answered automatically. She wondered if Bazzi had seen the kiss, then cringed. She had a real boyfriend, one working day and night at home to help her family. What would he say if he knew? Shame coursed through her.

"Mr. Bazzi is welcome to look for the manuscript whether Jake is there or not," she said. "So are you, Mr. —?"

"Tannous," the man said with a slight bow.

"Mr. Tannous. If someone finds the manuscript, could we buy it from them?"

"For the right price, perhaps. I would be happy to negotiate for you."

He got on the phone and had a long conversation in what Amy guessed was Koyra Chiini, the local town language. When he finished, he hung up and smiled. "It is all arranged."

"Is there something we can do for you?"

"If we are successful in procuring the manuscript, I would like a trip for my wife and me to Morocco, where we both have family."

"Agreed," Amy said. "My brother and his friend are on the other end of town, looking—"

"Yes, I know," Mr. Tannous interrupted. "The two boys." He laughed. "The younger one is claiming to be a student at Harvard University."

"That part is sort of true," Amy said.

"Remarkable!"

"I'll send the Mouse after them." She needed to warn them about the Wyomings and bring them back. With the twins in town, she didn't want Dan or Atticus out of her sight.

Amy ran outside to find the Mouse and tell Jake.

"Why are we here again?" Atticus asked.

"I want to pick up some things," Dan answered as he dodged people and goats in the crowded Grand Marché.

"Like what?"

"That depends on what they have."

Atticus stopped in the street so Dan was forced to turn around and look at him. The younger boy's eyes were unblinking behind his glasses. "You've been acting kind of strange since the camel head went missing. Are you sure you're okay?"

"I wish you'd stop asking that!" Dan snapped.

Atticus flinched as if he had been slapped. But Dan didn't care.

Atticus has no idea what's really going on. How long

it's been going on. Centuries. I need to gather the ingre-dients and take the formula. It's the only way to even the odds.

A worried Atticus followed Dan through the crowded market as he stopped at every stall, scanned the items for sale, then moved on to the next stall. "We could probably speed things along if you told me exactly what you're looking for," he said.

"It's hard to explain," Dan said. "I'll know it when I see it. What's this?" He was pointing at a stack of white slabs in different shapes and sizes.

"That would be salt," Atticus said.

Dan wrinkled his eyebrows. "That's what it looks like before it goes into a shaker?"

Atticus nodded. "This area is famous for its salt mines. People came here from all over the ancient world to get it. Without salt, they would have died. The Sahara used to be under the ocean, which is why . . . "

Atticus realized that he was talking to himself. Dan had moved on. He found him three stalls down, star-ing at dozens of open barrels filled with colorful herbs.

"Spices," Atticus said, keeping it simple so Dan didn't drift off again.

"I can't read the snake writing," Dan said. "Is there anything that says rosemary or mint?"

"Are you making spaghetti sauce for dinner?" Atticus asked. "Wanna go back and get some salt?"

"Very funny. Does he have them?"

Atticus read over the cards tacked to the barrels and nodded. "How much do you want?"

"A couple ounces of each should do it."

As Atticus spoke to the vendor, Dan idly scanned the crowd and noticed a man he thought he had seen outside the butcher shop. He wore a white robe and a red turban and kept his face covered. Dan couldn't be sure it was the same man, because half the people in the market were wearing robes and turbans.

Atticus handed him the spices. He put them in his pack and looked to see if the man was still there. He had disappeared.

"Ready to go?" Atticus asked.

"We might as well go up to the roof to see that view Bart was talking about."

"But the Vesp—"

"Trust me, I haven't forgotten," Dan cut him off. "It'll only take a minute." He hurried up the stairs.

The second-floor stalls had clothes, cheap jewelry, local crafts, artwork, antiques, and much more aggressive vendors.

"Buy this cheap!"

"Very rare!"

"For your mother!"

Dan went through the crowd quickly, ignoring the pitches, until he came to a stall hung with dozens of beautiful desert scenes. An old man stood in the corner in front of an easel painting. Unlike the other vendors, he barely gave them a second look when they walked in.

"Now you're an art collector?" Atticus asked.

"Get real." Dan rolled his eyes. "But I *am* interested in this." He was standing in front of a large painting of the Ishtar Gate, identical to the one at the Pergamon Museum, down to the compass rose beneath one of the oxen. "See the aurochs on the right-hand side?"

"I see them," Atticus said. "And I'm surprised you know that word."

Dan caught the sarcasm, but didn't blame him. "Everyone knows an aurochs is an extinct kind of oxen."

"In actuality, it's not an ox, it's a giant cow," Atticus responded. "They were close to six feet tall."

Dan ignored him. "Look at the giant, uh, bovine on the far right."

Atticus leaned in. "Whoa! The de Virga compass rose!"

They looked over at the old man. He had stopped painting and was staring at them with intense eyes.

"Do you speak English?" Atticus asked.

"And French, and German, and Spanish, and all the local dialects," came the man's calm reply. He walked out from behind the easel, wiping his hands on his paint-stained robe. "You're the two boys from the private jet looking for the manuscript."

"How did you—"

The artist waved him off. "Everyone in Timbuktu knows what you're doing here. I take it you didn't find it."

"Not yet," Dan said. "You painted this?"

"I painted all of them."

"It must be hard to make a living in Timbuktu as an artist," Atticus said.

"The only people who make a living at art in Timbuktu are con artists. I paint because I love it. I sell a few pieces here and there, but not the really good stuff."

"You've been in Timbuktu a long time?" Dan asked.

"I came here when I was nine years old. My father was a Persian diplomat and apparently not very popular, because he got sent here. He died when I was ten. My mother remarried into a wealthy local family and we stayed. I think you've met my son, Basharat."

"Bart?" Dan and Atticus said in unison.

"His street name. And you've also met my grandson. He is called the Mouse."

"I'm Dan Cahill and this is Atticus Rosenbloom."

"I am Mr. Tajamul." He gave them a slight bow. "You know, my son has been looking for you."

"Yeah, uh, we . . ." Dan didn't want to tell him that they had ditched him. He pointed at the painting of the Ishtar Gate. "So, you've been to Berlin."

Mr. Tajamul shook his head. "I haven't been out of Timbuktu since I was ten. I painted it from photographs."

"They must have been pretty detailed photographs. I just saw the wall yesterday, and this is a perfect replica, including this compass rose, which I bet most people standing right in front of it would miss."

"Do you mean Koldewey's mark?"

"The archaeologist?" Atticus asked.

"When I was a boy he stayed at our house when he was here on digs. He marked all of his discoveries with that compass rose. It wasn't clear in the photographs, but I knew what it was when I saw it. I've seen it before."

"Where?" Dan asked.

"At the dig outside town," Atticus said excitedly. "Robert Koldewey was an expert in excavating mudbrick houses, just like my dad!"

"I'll show you." Mr. Tajamul walked over to a stack of paintings leaning against a wall. "Here it is." He pulled a painting out and brought it back to them.

It was a painting of a half-buried town with sand blowing across the buildings. "As you can see, it was a walled city. It was a controversial dig because Koldewey was convinced that the town was of Roman origin. Unheard of in this part of Africa. He believed it was a salt-mining settlement for the Roman Empire."

"Roman as in Latin?" Dan asked.

"I suppose," Mr. Tajamul said. "That's what the Romans spoke."

He traced his paint-stained finger along the wall and stopped where he had painted the de Virga compass, or Koldewey's mark.

"Did they find any manuscripts there?" Dan asked.

He was nearly bouncing up and down from excitement.

"Not that I ever heard of. The town predates Timbuktu by hundreds of years."

"But the mark is still there."

"I'm certain it is," Mr. Tajamul said. "Koldewey made sure his marks were permanent. He knew what the ravages of time could do. The mark is also on the well in the center of the town. Koldewey died before he finished the dig. I think he knew the well was as far as he was going to get. He always put his mark on the edges, or the boundaries of his digs. He called them *die Fehlerspielräume*."

"What does that mean?" Dan asked.

A shocked Atticus translated. "It means 'margin for error.'"

Amy and Jake were searching through the five percent of manuscripts that Mr. Tannous had not digitized when Bart walked into the library. Alone.

"Where are they?" Amy asked.

"I was hoping they were here with you," Bart said.

Jake jumped to his feet. "You were supposed to watch them!"

Bart shrugged. "Difficult to watch two boys who do not want to be watched. The Mouse will find them."

Amy grabbed her pack and stood up. "No, we'll find them. We're going now."

"We better go," Dan said. "Thank you, Mr. Tajamul."

Mr. Tajamul gave them another bow, returned to his easel, and once more began to paint.

Dan and Atticus did not get very far. Standing outside the stall was the white-robed, red-turbaned man Dan had seen outside the butcher shop. Except he wasn't a local. Casper Wyoming was holding the

Mouse trapped in one hand and a shiny curved dagger in the other.

"Casper!" Atticus screamed.

"Let him go!" Dan said, his mouth going as dry the desert.

"There's a wonderful knife maker here," Casper said, increasing the blade's pressure on the Mouse's neck, causing the boy to squirm. "His blades are razor-sharp. Deadly. Cheyenne was so impressed she decided to get one as well. She's waiting at the bottom of the stairs with her own knife. A twin to this, so to speak."

"The Mouse has nothing to do with this," Dan said.

Casper responded by increasing the blade's pressure until it bit into the boy's neck. "Squeak, squeak," Casper said. The Mouse's eyes were wide with fear.

"What do you want?" Dan asked. His heart was booming in his ears. The afternoon sun beat down on the silver of the knife, flashing into his eyes until the bright white light was all he could see.

"I only caught bits and pieces of your conversation with the old man. Tell me what you learned or I'll cut this little rodent into pieces."

Dan desperately looked up and down the aisle for help, but the vendors were all in their stalls. No one was paying attention.

"Why do you care?" he demanded. "If we find what Vesper One's looking for, we're going to turn it over to you anyway."

"My sister and I would prefer to find it ourselves."

Casper smiled. "We want to *cut* you out of the deal." He glanced at the terrified boy. "And whoever else gets in our way. Vesper One doesn't trust you. He thinks you might be holding back."

Dan had no choice. He was about to tell Casper about the Koldewey mark when an idea came to him. He reached into his pocket.

"Hold it!" Casper growled.

"It's my cell phone," Dan said. "Do you want the information or not?"

"What's it have to do with your phone?"

"I recorded what he told us so I could download it for Amy," Dan said, trying to find enough spit to speak. "I wasn't able to send it because there isn't any signal. Ready?"

Casper nodded.

Dan hoped this worked. If it didn't, he would be responsible for another death, this time of a little kid. He turned the volume up as high as it would go and hit the icon. His ringtone blared across the second floor, down the stairs to the first, and out the window to the street. The Grand Marché went wild. Every vendor jumped out of their stall, brandishing their cell phones. A stampede of people rushed up the stairs, crushing Casper in the desperate race to catch Dan's fake signal. The Mouse pulled out of Casper's grasp and darted away through the limbs and arms of the shouting mass.

"This way!" The Mouse pointed to the stairs leading to the roof.

Dan poked his head into Mr. Tajamul's stall. He was still at his easel, painting, seemingly oblivious to the riot outside.

Mr. Tajamul looked at him. "Bars?"

"No!" Dan shouted. "There's a maniac out here who's going to torture you for information when he gets back on his feet."

Mr. Tajamul threw his brush down and ran out of the stall.

Dan was right behind him. Casper was up on his hands and knees now, with a bloody nose as red as the turban on his head. He looked like an enraged lion ready to pounce.

Dan fought his way up the stairs against the flow. When he finally reached the roof he found Atticus standing at the edge. Alone.

"Where's the Mouse?"

Atticus pointed. The Mouse was standing on the roof of the building next to the Grand Marché, frantically motioning them to join him. Between the buildings was a ten-foot gap and a two-story drop.

"I can't jump that!" Atticus said, turning terrified eyes toward Dan.

Dan wasn't sure if he could, either. He looked behind and saw to his horror that Casper had regained his feet and was limping toward them. Cheyenne, dressed exactly like her brother, was not limping. She was sprinting toward them at a dead run with her twin dagger glinting in the setting sun's light.

Dan grabbed Atticus, pulled him fifteen feet back from the edge, and shouted, "Run!"

Atticus looked behind him, saw Cheyenne, and took off as if he were on fire. He cleared the gap with feet to spare. Dan had a second to marvel at what pure fear could do before it was his turn to jump. He barely made it. At the very last moment Cheyenne's dagger split his shirt down the back.

Dan got shakily to his feet, worried that his adrenaline-saturated heart was going to pound out of his chest.

"She's going to jump!" Atticus shouted.

Cheyenne had backed away from the edge and was making her run. Just as she reached the edge of the Grand Marché, her foot got tangled in her robe. She dropped into the gap like a skydiver with a collapsed chute.

Dan, Atticus, and the Mouse peered over the edge. They were only slightly disappointed. Cheyenne was alive, but she had landed in an enormous mound of camel dung. She was clutching her arm and grimacing in pain.

"See you later," Dan jeered.

The words were only just out of his mouth when Casper's dagger came whistling past Dan's ear. It missed him by inches and stuck in a wooden beam with a loud *twang*.

Casper looked at him and smiled. "Better run, little boys. You only have a few more hours."

CHAPTER 27

"Luna doesn't seem too paranoid about being followed," Jonah said.

She was a half a block ahead of them, walking at a leisurely pace as if she were taking a stroll through a well-lit mall.

"I hear you," Hamilton said. "She hasn't even looked back to see if anyone is behind her."

"It's probably because she's packin' heat." Jonah looked at his giant cousin. "That means carrying a gun."

"I know what packing heat is!" Hamilton said. "Like you know anything about guns."

"Dude! Didn't you see me in my number-one-grossing box-office hit, *Gangsta Kronikles*?"

"No," Hamilton lied.

"Well, you're probably the only dude on the planet who hasn't seen it. I was the bomb in that movie and it was no act. Some things you just can't fake. If the bad guys I wasted in the movie had been real we wouldn't have an overpopulation problem on Planet E."

"Whatever."

Luna led them past the massive stone walls of Mahim Fort, then turned left toward the bay and entered what smelled and looked like a fishing village. They lost sight of her among the dilapidated shacks. Unlike on the street, there were a lot of people hanging around outside their homes, making it difficult for Hamilton and Jonah to remain inconspicuous.

"Where'd she go?" Jonah asked.

"Jonah Wizard!" a girl yelled from behind them.

Jonah took off at a sprint without even bothering to turn and look back. He and Hamilton dashed through the maze of shacks, ending up on a muddy bank near the bay where a group of fishermen was standing around a fire, laughing uproariously. The uproar turned to menace when the men saw the out-of-breath boys appear out of nowhere. One of the fishermen was dressed like Luna Amato.

"It was a ruse!" Hamilton said.

The men started moving toward them. Their laughter had been replaced by a terrifying silence. Behind them an army of young fans started pouring out of the fishing village, brandishing camera phones and shouting, "Jonah! Jonah! Jonah!"

Jonah looked around frantically, his eyes zeroing in on the only possible escape. "Boat!" The rap star had a lot of experience getting away from rushing crowds.

They sprinted into the water and jumped into the first boat they reached.

"I'll pull up the anchor," Jonah shouted. "You start the motor."

"There is no motor!" Hamilton yelled.

"Hoist the sail!"

The wind caught the sail just as the fake Luna Amato reached the gunwale and started to pull himself up. Hamilton grabbed an oar and knocked him back into the water.

Jonah took the rudder and swung the bow around as Hamilton peeled two more people off the side and they splashed down into the water. The boat started to move out into Mahim Bay, leaving the fans and the angry fishermen shouting from the shallows.

Hamilton pulled his cell phone out and turned it on. "That was a trap! We have to warn Erasmus." He listened, then shook his head. "Voice mail."

"We have to get back there!" Jonah swung the boat south. "Could you recognize the warehouse from here?"

Hamilton shook his head. "Not in the dark. But Erasmus said Mahim Fort was a couple miles from the warehouse. All we have to do is figure out where two miles is and ground this thing." He narrowed his eyes at Jonah. "Where'd you learn to sail?"

"Video game."

Hamilton rolled his eyes. "Let me take the rudder."

"Word."

They switched places. "One more question," Hamilton said.

"Give it to me."

"What does *word* mean?"

"Literal translation?"

"Yeah."

"It means, 'Okay, I agree, hey.'"

"All three of those things?"

"Word."

Casper Wyoming limped into the alley. He found his sister picking camel dung off her green-streaked robe with her good hand.

"I think my arm is broken," she said. "What's the matter with you?"

"I twisted my ankle."

"That's not what I meant and you know it! Vesper One told us to leave the Cahills alone."

"He told us to keep an eye on them and not to impede them in any way. I grabbed the rodent boy, not the Cahill brats. It looked to me like you were trying to impede them with that dagger."

"I wasn't trying to *impede* them," Cheyenne said. "I was trying to *impale* them."

They glared at each other for a moment, then Casper started chuckling.

"You better hope Vesper One doesn't get wind of what happened," Cheyenne said, her eyes narrowing.

"He won't." Casper glanced over his shoulder. "This place has one thing going for it." He smiled. "It's great for making people disappear."

CHAPTER 28

"There!"

Amy pointed at the three boys jogging down the street.

Atticus and Dan piled into the backseat. The Mouse squeezed in next to Amy in the front.

Bart reached around Amy and ruffled his son's hair. "What kind of trouble have you been in?"

The Mouse only grinned.

"Where have you been?" Amy demanded. "We were worried sick."

"Fighting off the evil twins," Dan said.

"The Wyomings!" Amy paled. "Are you all right?"

"Yeah, but Tweedledumb and Tweedledemented are a little worse for wear. Cheyenne did a header into a pile of camel poop."

"We never should have let them go off on their own," Jake said, staring daggers at Amy.

Amy glared right back. "If you hadn't—"

"If we hadn't gone off on our own," Dan interrupted, "we wouldn't have figured out where the 'Apology' is."

"You know where it is?" Amy asked, turning to her brother with a gasp of astonishment.

"The de Virga compass rose hasn't let us down yet." He told her about the Roman ruins. "You and Jake can continue with the manuscripts. Atticus and I will head out to the ruins and see where it leads us."

"Forget it," Jake said. "Every time we leave you two on your own it leads to disaster."

"I agree with Dan," Atticus said. "If Koldewey was right about it being a Roman settlement, it's the only place in the Sahara Desert that has a chance of having something written in Latin."

"There's only one problem with your theory. The ancient town you're talking about is half-buried underneath the Sahara Desert," Jake pointed out.

"Everyone in Timbuktu is searching here for the manuscripts," Amy said. She told them about her deal with Mr. Tannous. "We should cover all possible angles." She looked at her watch. "And we only have a few hours."

"Perfect," Dan said. "Let's head out to the ruins." He tapped Bart on the shoulder. "Do you have a shovel in the trunk?"

"I cannot drive you to the ruins in my taxi," Bart said. "The only way to get there is on foot or on ships of the desert."

"Ships of the desert?" Amy asked.

Atticus gave a fist pump. "He means camels!"

CHAPTER 29

Yes.

Amy's answer hadn't really mattered. Erasmus was going to break into the Vesper safe house no matter what she said. But he'd checked it with her anyway out of consideration for Grace Cahill. Grace had picked Amy to lead the Cahills for a reason and so far, the girl was doing a fine job. She deserved a little respect.

Erasmus knew the person leaving the warehouse was not Luna Amato. He'd sent Jonah and Hamilton after the imposter, hoping to convince Luna that her ruse had worked. Now he slipped on a pair of enhanced night-vision goggles and scanned the building's windows. There was no movement, no flash of light behind the dark panes, but he did discover something useful. On the second floor, to the right of the entrance, was a window that wasn't latched. It made no difference to him whether Luna still was inside or not, but he didn't want her to know that *he* was. He would search the warehouse undetected.

He checked his pockets to make sure everything was in place. He had spent many years in Japan when he was young and had been thoroughly trained in ninjutsu. His black leather getup was not to protect him from a motorcycle accident, nor was it a fashion statement. It was designed to protect, to defend — and to make him invisible.

He glided across the street and scaled the drainage pipe to the second floor as quietly and efficiently as a vine snake. Before opening the window, he sprayed each hinge with a special brew of lubricants and graphite. The window opened without a whisper. He was through in an instant. The first thing he noticed was the air-conditioning. Not only was it cool, there wasn't a speck of dust floating past the lenses of his goggles.

Sixty-five degrees. Filtered air. Environmentally sealed.

The second floor was made up of a single room two hundred feet wide by three hundred feet deep, with enclosed cubicles scattered around the perimeter. In the center of the room was a huge freight elevator with a forklift parked next to it. Next to the elevator was a set of stairs.

The outside may be five hundred years old, but the guts are five years old. Maximum.

He started checking out the cubicles. The first one had a jeweler's bench and all the equipment needed to cut precious stones. Above the wall were detailed photographs and drawings of the Golden Jubilee Diamond.

The next cubicle smelled of oil paint and ink. A partially completed masterpiece in the style of Vincent van Gogh sat on an easel. It was a work Erasmus didn't recognize. He could see the headline now: "Undiscovered Van Gogh sells for millions at auction."

Across from the easel was a workbench with stacks of etched currency plates, euros, dollars, yen . . . denominations from almost every country. In the next cubicle were a state-of-the-art printing press and crates of bundled cash.

Vespers make their money by making their own money, Erasmus noted.

In the third cubicle he found what looked like the model Antikythera Mechanism, stolen from the American Computer Museum. It was difficult to tell because it had been disassembled, with the pieces spread out on a long stainless-steel table. Above the pieces was a photo of the original Antikythera fragment. Again it looked familiar to Erasmus, but he still couldn't place it. He walked over to a stack of schematics. The top plan was for a gigantic electromagnet, bigger than the one stolen in France. *Are the Vespers using the stolen French electromagnet for parts? What does the Antikythera Mechanism have to do with all of this?*

Erasmus had learned more about the Vespers in the last ten minutes than he had learned in the last ten years. His brain buzzed with information and plans. He decided that he would disturb nothing in the warehouse. Instead he would stay in Mumbai and watch it, find out who worked here, track the shipments in and out. No doubt Vesper One had several warehouses like this, probably in different countries, but it might take him years to find them.

A frightening question occurred to him.

Why had Luna sent a decoy out? She had to know that she was being followed.

He heard a door open on the first floor. Whoever opened it had done so quietly, but not nearly quietly enough. Were the footsteps Luna's? Or someone else's?

Erasmus glided out of the cubicle and took up a position behind the forklift with a clear view of the stairway. If Luna turned on the lights, it was all over for him. He was too far away from the window to use it as an exit. A flashlight beam danced up through the dark. The light bounced off a white wall and illuminated a man's profile.

Milos Vanek!

The Interpol agent had a flashlight in one hand and a pistol in the other.

"Dude. We've gone two miles," Jonah insisted.

Hamilton wasn't so sure, but he swung the bow toward shore anyway, hoping they didn't smash into a bunch of sharp rocks.

"Can you swim?" he asked.

"I'm a fish."

The boat lurched to a sudden stop and Jonah was catapulted off the bow.

"You okay?" Hamilton yelled.

"Word!"

Hamilton made a perfect dive off the gunwale and started swimming. To his surprise, Jonah was right behind him when he reached the shore.

Agent Vanek paused on the second floor only long enough to give it a cursory sweep with his flashlight before continuing up.

He must have followed us to the warehouse.

Erasmus had to give the inspector his due. He had looked for a tail when they were following Luna and hadn't spotted him. He wondered if Vanek had followed the fake Luna, or if he had just waited outside and watched Erasmus scale the downspout.

But it didn't matter. Erasmus had no intention of letting Vanek spot him again.

There was a crash and dull thud from the third floor. Every muscle in Erasmus's body tensed. He heard someone dragging something, or someone, across the floor. He hoped Vanek wasn't the one being dragged.

I can't get involved.

Erasmus was on a mission. Agent Vanek's agenda was not his concern.

A light came on. A woman's voice began to speak.

Despite himself, Erasmus crept closer to the stairway to listen.

"Vanek, you are old, and slow, and not too smart. So sorry about your head, but that will not matter in a moment. Did you not think I noticed you and your friends following me? A motorcycle, a taxi, and a rickshaw? You have lost your edge."

Erasmus heard a slap and a moan.

I can't get involved.

"Interpol is on its way," Vanek said.

"Really? Let me see your cell phone. Ah yes . . . here we go. It seems that your smartphone is smarter than you. It does not lie. You made a call to Interpol over two hours ago. Since then no incoming calls, no texts, no outgoing e-mail. Interpol has no idea where you are. Perhaps you had plans for me you did not want them to know about, hmm?"

There was a pause, and Erasmus could picture Luna's smug expression. "They will find you floating on your belly in Mahim Bay, or perhaps in two days in the Arabian Sea a little worse for wear from sharks. I am the judge, the jury, and the executioner. Does the convicted have anything to say before I carry out the sentence?"

I can't get involved.

"You are a traitor, Luna Amato."

"Is that the best you can do? A pathetic end to a pathetic life. Good-bye, Milos Va—"

As quick and quiet as a cat, Erasmus was at the top

of the stairs with a throwing dart in hand. The iron *bo shuriken* struck Luna's gun hand before she could finish Vanek's last name. Erasmus swept her feet out from under her, kicking her gun down the stairs in one fluid motion. Then he picked up Vanek's gun and aimed it at her with frozen eyes.

Luna held up a bloody hand to shield herself. "You don't understand, Erasmus," she pleaded. "Yours are not the only hostages the Vespers are keeping!"

Erasmus looked at Vanek. A bruise was forming on his cheek. Blood ran from his nose. Luna had handcuffed him to a chair. "You okay?"

"Yes," a shaken Vanek answered.

Erasmus watched as Luna got unsteadily to her feet. He had never knocked an old woman down, but had absolutely no regrets about it. Luna Amato was as dangerous as a viper.

"The Vespers have my son," she said. "They threatened to kill him if I didn't help."

"Don't listen to her," Vanek shouted. "Luna does not have a son!"

"And Vanek is a liar! He put Amy and Dan in a Turkish prison to rot. It was I who got them out! It is Vanek who is working for the Vespers."

"I don't even know what a Vesper is," Vanek said.

Erasmus looked toward Vanek. It was only a split second, but it was enough.

The viper struck. Erasmus saw Luna's hand move, but it was too late. The *bo shuriken* was streaking through the air like a bullet. It sliced through his leather vest as if it were soft cheese and buried itself in his heart. He clutched his chest with both hands. His knees buckled and he dropped to the wooden floor. He could not believe that the last thing he was going to see on Earth was the gloating face of an evil old woman.

Luna snatched the gun off the floor with her good hand and pointed it at him. "In three minutes this building will be rubble, but you will not hear the explosion. The pleasure of killing you will be mine."

"No!"

Jonah Wizard flew into the room, with Vanek's lost gun steady in his hands. He fired three times—*Bam! Bam! Bam!*—hitting Luna Amato in the torso at point-blank range. But this was not *Gangsta Kronikles* or his other action movies. The bullets were not blanks. They knocked her backward into the wall, where she slid to the floor, a look of shock and terror on her old face.

Jonah stared in horror at her—at what he had done to her.

He was no longer Jonah Wizard, platinum-selling recording artist and movie star.

He was Jonah Wizard, murderer.

Hamilton ran over to Erasmus and tried to stanch the blood pumping out of his chest. "I'll call an ambulance."

Erasmus shook his head. "Too late. In my pocket . . . Thumb drive. Hurry."

Hamilton fumbled with the zipper slick with blood and pulled it out.

"Give it to Amy. Only Amy."

"Okay," Hamilton mumbled.

"Take all the cell phones. Do a data dump to Attleboro. Get out of here. Safe house on my phone . . . In London. Hide. . . . The Vespers are . . ."

But Erasmus didn't have the breath to finish his sentence. His chest gave a great shudder and then he was gone.

Jonah stood over them. He could barely speak. "Is he . . . ?"

"He's dead," Hamilton said, his big face streaked with tears.

"You must go," Vanek said. "Luna said the building is going to explode. It was a trap."

Hamilton nodded dully and picked up the cell phones. "Where are the keys to the handcuffs?"

"There is not time," Vanek said. "Leave me!"

Hamilton handed the cell phones to a silent Jonah. He picked up Vanek, chair and all, and hurried down the stairs.

Hamilton set the chair, with Vanek still attached to it, down in the alley just as the explosion ripped through the night air.

"Call the police. I will explain everything to them," Vanek said. "They will not keep you too long."

"They won't be keeping us at all," Hamilton said. "We're leaving."

"No! You do not understand. I am on your side. If you will just call, I will—"

Hamilton shook his head. "You don't understand. We're leaving. You're staying."

Vanek fixed Hamilton with his cool blue gaze. "What is happening to you children? Who is doing this to you?"

Hamilton ignored him. "We'll give the police a call once we're clear." He looked at Jonah. "You want to drive?"

Jonah shook his head and climbed into the back of the rickshaw.

"Are you okay?" Hamilton asked, expecting Jonah to say, "Word."

But Jonah had sunk somewhere deep inside himself. He said nothing at all.

CHAPTER 30

Riding a camel was just as uncomfortable as it had always looked in the movies to Dan. Bart had gone to the camel market and rented three of the cantankerous beasts. Dan rode with Atticus behind Bart and his son, whose real name they learned was Aza, which meant "comfort." Amy and Jake were on the third camel in the rear.

"I don't know why they call them ships of the desert," Dan said. "This is nothing like sailing. It's like riding a category-six rapid in slow motion. I think a kidney just dropped out of my pant leg."

Atticus laughed.

Amy smiled. The ride on the third camel was just as bumpy, but it didn't bother her. She had her arms wrapped around Jake's waist to steady her.

"I might have been wrong about the margin," Jake said.

"We don't know that yet."

"I just hope Dan has it right," Jake said. He leaned back against her and looked up at the bright stars against the black sky. The desert stretched all around the small group, vast and peaceful. And yet the Cahills could only think of the clock ticking ever forward, of the seven lives on the line.

By the time they arrived at the ruin, there was only an hour and a half left before Vesper One's deadline.

"If we found the 'Apology' right this minute, we wouldn't have time to get it back to Timbuktu," Amy said to Jake.

"Vesper One didn't say where we had to deliver it," Jake pointed out. "He just said we had to *find* it."

"This is the outer wall of the city," Bart said. "Aza says that he and his friends come here all the time. He knows the place well."

"Then he's our official tour guide," Dan said.

They grabbed flashlights and started following the decaying wall with Aza and Bart in the lead.

"Here it is!" Bart called out.

They ran up to him.

The compass rose was carved into the mud-brick wall, just as Mr. Tajamul had painted it.

"You were right, Dan," Amy said. "It matches the de Virga! But what does it mean?"

They spent ten valuable minutes searching along the city wall, but all they found was sand and two scorpions, which they were all careful not to step on.

Atticus gave the second scorpion a dubious look.

"Did you know more people are killed by scorpions than snakes? I hear it's a very painful way to go."

This sort of talk was normally right up Dan's alley, but even he seemed entirely focused on the approaching deadline. "C'mon!" he said, ignoring Atticus. "We have to check out the second Koldewey mark."

It took them twenty precious minutes to reach the well.

"Koldewey's mark," Atticus said. "Exactly like the other one."

Dan shined his light down the well. "It's only about four feet deep. It must be filled with sand." His whole body slumped.

"Think!" Amy said. "We have forty minutes left!"

Jake walked very slowly around the well, covering every square inch with his flashlight. Then he shined the light down the well's opening, circling it once again, leaning over to peer in.

"Thirty-five minutes," Amy said.

Jake popped his head out of the opening. "It's not a well!"

"What is it?" Dan asked.

"It's an air vent."

"How do you know?"

"Because my dad's an archaeologist, and I've been on dozens of digs. The wall around is too high for a well and the opening is too narrow."

"An air vent for what?" Amy asked, excitement growing in her voice.

"An ancient mine," Jake replied. "There's an opening on the side near the bottom. They built them this way so water didn't flow into the shaft."

"I'll go check it out," Dan said, and threw his leg over the side.

"Me first," Jake said, pushing him aside. "I'm taller. There's no telling how far the drop is to the mine floor. If it's safe I'll give you a shout."

He started to climb into the opening. Amy put her hand on his shoulder. "Be careful."

Jake shot her a grin, then disappeared.

They waited an anxious few minutes before Jake called up, his voice echoing hollowly against the rock of the shaft. "It's safe!"

Dan jumped down the hole like a rabbit. Amy and Atticus followed, leaving Bart and Aza behind.

The tunnel was only five feet tall, so the only one who didn't have to stoop was Atticus. He shined his light on the walls. "There's Latin graffiti!"

"Anything good?" Dan asked.

"Just your run-of-the-mill bathroom humor."

"The tunnel's collapsed just beyond the vent," Jake said. "But we can go the other way."

As they followed him down the tunnel, Atticus

skimmed the walls for the words *apology* or *transgression*. The others crowded around him, but he didn't find anything.

Amy looked at her watch. "We only have twenty-five minutes!"

"There's a room up ahead," Jake said.

They hurried forward. The small room was built into the side of the tunnel before the tunnel continued on. Inside were two raised platforms of different heights, and leaning against the wall were slabs of salt like Dan and Atticus had seen at the Grand Marché.

"Is it a storage room?" Amy asked.

"I don't think so." Jake shined his light on the lower platform. "I think this is a bed. And the other one is a worktable." He pointed his flashlight above the table. "It's definitely some kind of table. See the torches?" He reached up to a piece of wood sticking out of the wall and touched it. "Charcoal. This was someone's hideaway. Someone important. It wouldn't have been easy to build. They wouldn't give a slave a room like this." He walked over to the opening and shined his light around the edge. "Hinge marks. There used to be a door here, and probably a lock as well. They wouldn't lock up salt slabs. The salt was only valuable when it got to market. It was worthless out here in the desert."

"I think I found something!" Dan called.

He was looking at one of the salt slabs.

"It's just salt," Amy said.

"I know what it is," Dan said. "I just went through

every slab in here, but this one's different. There's something carved on it."

Jake carefully blew the sand off the surface. "Dan's right! There are words, and they're in Latin." He turned to Atticus. "Your Latin is better than mine."

Atticus tried to get the right angle with his flashlight. "It's hard to read in this light, but it's a long piece of writing. It must have taken forever to carve."

"We only have fifteen minutes!" Amy cried.

"It was written by a centurion named Gaius Marius. The first line reads *'apologia pro meus valde delictum.'* It's the 'Apology!'"

The little group collapsed in relief.

"Wow," Dan said.

Amy looked at her watch. "With thirteen minutes to spare!" She threw her arms around Dan and Atticus and hugged them both, much to their disgust.

"Why would anyone write on a salt tablet?" Jake asked.

Amy remembered what Bazzi had said. "In the ancient world, paper was worth more than gold. That's why scholars wrote in the margins of the manuscripts."

Atticus pored over the tablet. "The centurion says that he volunteered to come out here in 'self-exile' to do 'penance' for murdering a great man and stealing an invention, or some kind of machine from him. Apparently he was in charge of the salt mine. Below the writing is a drawing. I can't make it out in this light."

"Yoo-hoo!" A familiar and horrible voice echoed

down the tunnel. "Olly olly oxen free!"

Atticus flinched.

"Cheyenne," Amy said. "How'd she find us?"

"We have your friends," Cheyenne shouted. "Do you have something for us?"

"Leave them alone!" Amy shouted back. "They have nothing to do with this and we have"—Amy looked at her watch—"ten minutes!"

"Casper says that you have five minutes. And that he hates mice, so the little boy goes first."

"Can you translate the rest of it in five minutes?" Amy asked Atticus.

"Are you kidding?" Atticus squeaked. "It would take me at least five hours under perfect lighting conditions. And then there's the carving."

"Take a photo of it with your camera phone."

Dan shot a quick photo, but the results were a white blurry blob of nothing.

"Tick-tock, tick-tock," Cheyenne cooed.

"Wait!" Amy shouted back. "It's connected to the tunnel wall. I don't think Vesper One would be too happy if we destroyed it."

"I guess we have to give it to them without reading it," Dan said.

"No, we don't," Jake said. He looked at Atticus. "Do you have paper in your pack?"

"Of course, but I told you, I can't do a trans—"

"We'll do a rubbing," Jake said.

Atticus looked at him in despair. "We don't have

charcoal."

Jake stood up and pulled the old torch out of the wall. "Yes, we do."

Atticus tore sheets of paper out of the notebook he always carried and slapped them on the slab.

"How long will this take?" Amy asked.

"Three or four minutes."

"I'll go up and see if I can stall them."

"I'll go with you," Dan said.

Casper had the dagger in his hand. Bart and Aza were on their knees in front of him with their hands tied behind their backs. Aza was cowering into his father's side, and Bart was doing his best to inch his son behind him.

"They climbed down a ladder from the sky," Bart said. "And were on us before I could do anything."

"It's not your fault," Amy said, tears pricking behind her eyes. "I'm so sorry."

"Shut up," Casper said. "Do you have the 'Apology'?"

"Jake's bringing it. It's heavy."

"What's it written on?" Cheyenne asked.

"Salt."

Dan's head appeared from the hole and his eyes flashed over to Bart and Aza. "Don't worry. The thing they want is right behind me."

"It better be, or a lot of your friends are going to die," said Cheyenne. She looked at Bart.

Atticus emerged from the hole next. Dan helped

him over the lip.

"Where's your brother?" Casper asked.

"Right behind me."

Jake appeared with the salt slab. He balanced the 'Apology' on the edge as he hoisted himself out.

Cheyenne rushed over and looked at the slab with her flashlight. "It's in Latin."

"This thing's heavy," Jake said. "You're going to have a hard time lifting it with one arm."

"I'll manage." She reached for the slab.

Jake tipped it toward the opening. "Careful."

"What are you doing, you idiot?" Cheyenne shrieked.

Jake ignored her and looked at Casper. "Cut them loose."

"You're in no position to dictate anything to us," Casper said. "You're forgetting that we have your friends. One call from me and a hostage dies."

"You know what?" Jake said, his face like granite. "They're not my friends. I've never even met them. But I do know that man and that boy. Free them or I'm going to tip this slab right back into the pit."

"Jake!" Amy shouted. But the harsh look froze what she was going to say on her tongue.

"You wouldn't," Cheyenne said.

"Really?" Jake tipped the slab.

"Stop!" Casper said. With a quick sweep of his knife, he cut Bart's and Aza's flex-cuffs.

"Get the camels ready," Jake said.

Bart and Aza untied the camels and made them

koosh, or lie down.

"Mount up," Jake said. "Here's how we're going to work this. I'll be the last man on the camel. I'm going to take my hand off the slab and you're going to have to balance it or it's going to fall. It weighs over seventy pounds and it's slick. You can't lift it by yourself with one arm." He looked over at the camels. Everybody was on board. "Here you go."

He took his hand away and Cheyenne barely caught it. Casper rushed over to help her.

"See you later," Jake said, swinging up in front of Amy.

Bart gave the command for *up*. The camels got to their feet and the small group took off at a run.

Behind them, Dan could see Casper pick up the heavy slab and walk off into the darkness with it.

"They must have a four-wheeler," Amy said. They listened for the start of an engine, but there wasn't a sound.

"Oh, one more thing," Cheyenne said. Her voice came from somewhere above them.

"What the—" Dan couldn't believe his ears.

"It was a ladder in the sky," Bart insisted.

They looked up and saw an airship silhouetted against the stars.

"Remember this," Cheyenne continued, "and then there were six."

She and Casper started laughing.

"And then there were six!" Her voice faded away as the airship rose. "And then there were six!"

CHAPTER 31

Evan Tolliver was asleep with his face on his keyboard after a miserable evening of trying to reach Amy without success. He woke up and stumbled into the comm center bathroom to wash his face. As badly as he wanted to hear from Amy, he hoped she didn't Skype him until after the key dents faded from his forehead. He came back out and went directly to the espresso machine even though the last thing he needed was another shot of caffeine.

But coffee is the only thing keeping me functional. He rubbed his bloodshot eyes. *Barely functional.*

He stirred in a scoop of artificial creamer and way too much sugar and brought the golden elixir back to his computer terminal. As he was sitting down, the phone rang. Hot coffee spilled all over his hand and lap. He leaped up and grabbed the Bluetooth off the desk as he shook his scalded hand and tried to pull his boiling underpants away from his skin.

"Yes?" he growled.

"It's Hamilton."

Evan was glad it wasn't Amy. After their last conversation, the last thing he wanted to do was snap at her.

"How's Mumbai?"

"We're leaving."

"What about Luna?"

"She's dead."

"What?"

"D-E-A-D."

"I heard you," Evan said, forgetting all about his burns. First McIntyre and now Luna. Before he'd met Amy, he'd never known anyone who had died. Not even a distant relative. "How?"

"Jonah shot her."

Evan sat back down.

"Are you there?" Hamilton asked.

"I'm here." Evan had never shot a gun.

"There's worse news. Much worse." Hamilton hesitated. "Luna killed . . . Luna killed Erasmus."

A wave of dizziness washed over Evan, and he couldn't quite figure out how to respond. He had never met Erasmus, but he'd e-mailed him dozens of times each day. He'd become very fond of him through their exchanges. From what everyone had told him, Erasmus was an awesome guy.

"I'm so sorry," Evan said. It sounded pitifully inadequate, but he didn't know what else to say.

"It was horrible," Hamilton said, his deep voice cracking. "But I can't think about it right now. Just before he died, Erasmus asked me to do a data dump."

"What kind of data dump?"

"From three cell phones. Erasmus's, Luna Amato's, and Milos Vanek's."

"Agent Vanek was there?"

"Yeah. We left him in the alley. It's a long story. I don't have time for the details. We're about ready to take off."

"Okay." Evan forced himself to concentrate on the data. "Plug the phones into a computer and download the information. It's easy. I'll walk you through it."

"I don't have a computer."

Evan frowned. "I'm sure there's one on Jonah's jet."

"We're not on his jet. We're on a commercial flight in coach."

"Coach?" Evan blinked. "People must be going crazy with Jonah Wizard in the cheap seats."

"They don't know he's here. I got him pretty well disguised. He's barely spoken since he shot Luna. I'm worried. I think he's gone off the deep end," Hamilton said. "Oh, no," he groaned. "They've closed the door and are making us turn off our cell phones."

"Wait! Where are you headed?"

"I better not say. Talk to you later."

The line went dead.

Evan ran downstairs. He had to tell Sinead what had happened. Ian was sitting on the sofa with a Bluetooth in his good ear and a laptop on his lap.

"What's the hurry?" Ian asked.

Evan glared at him. He wasn't about to tell Ian anything. "Nothing," he said.

Ian pointed at his pants. "You need to time your bathroom breaks better."

"It's coffee!"

"Right."

"What are *you* doing?"

"Working, as you can see. Someone has to figure this whole thing out. And I'm making some progress."

Someone has to prove that you're a traitorous swine.

Evan cut through the kitchen, which was the shortest route to the guesthouse in back. Saladin slipped through the door as he opened it. He didn't think about it until he heard Ian scream from the living room. Normally that would have made him laugh, but he was too stressed out to even smile.

Erasmus is dead.

He couldn't believe it. He hurried across the backyard to the small house and burst through the front door without bothering to knock.

Sinead was sitting at her desk, working on her laptop. She snapped it shut and turned around. "What's happened?"

"Erasmus is dead! Amy's in Timbuktu! Hamilton and Jonah are on the run!"

"You better sit down and take a breath," Sinead said. "Start from the beginning."

CHAPTER 32

It was almost five in the morning by the time Amy, Dan, Atticus, and Jake arrived at the Timbuktu airport. They were exhausted, but pleased. So were Mr. and Mrs. Tannous. Even though the 'Apology' hadn't been found in the manuscripts, Amy wanted to repay Mr. Tannous's kindness with a ride to Morocco.

"Where to?" the pilot asked.

"Morocco," Amy said. "After we get there we'll let you know where we need to go next. Do we have Wi-Fi?"

"We will when we reach altitude."

As soon as they were up in the air, Atticus and Dan unbuckled and started laying the rubbings out on the floor.

Dan stared at his cell phone, waiting for a signal. At twenty thousand feet the bars went full. He got a text, but it wasn't from AJT. It was from Sinead.

```
Erasmus dead. Luna Amato dead. I have
proof that Ian is the traitor. Have Amy
call or Skype me ASAP.
```

Dan stared blankly at his phone, as if he couldn't quite arrange the letters in his mind. As if something so awful couldn't possibly be real.

Erasmus dead. He can't be dead.

He walked back to where Amy was sitting. She was booting up her laptop, fussing through her papers the way she liked. For once she looked calm, relaxed, as if every waking second of their lives wasn't a walking crisis. And Dan was going to shatter her hard-won calm.

"Amy?" he said, reaching down to touch his sister's shoulder. And then he broke the news.

Amy had to read the text several times before the information fully computed. Her brother was sitting in the seat across from her, staring at the blackness out the window with hollow eyes.

"This can't be true," Amy said. "It simply can't be true."

Tears streamed down her face. *I sent him into the stronghold. I said yes. I'm responsible for his death.*

A Skype call came in on her laptop and she picked up automatically. Ian Kabra's face filled the screen.

"Hi, Amy," he said cheerfully. "Where are you?"

"You know exactly where I am," Amy answered, a storm of raw fury building in her chest.

"Actually, I don't," Ian said. "The reason I'm calling is to tell I've made some progress. My mother is—"

"How could you do this?" Amy screamed. "How could you do this to your own sister?"

"What are you talking about? I'm trying to find out where Natalie is, just like you—"

"Erasmus is dead!"

"Erasmus is what?"

"I hate you, Ian Kabra!" Amy slammed the laptop closed so hard that the screen shattered.

The Vesper phone rang. Amy grabbed it from her bag and nearly smashed it, too. She took a deep breath and pushed the button. A photograph appeared. The hostages. They looked terrible. Nellie's jumpsuit was torn to shreds and her face and arm were swollen. Alistair Oh's jumpsuit was torn as well, and there was blood on his exposed knee. All of them appeared to have injuries except for Ted Starling and . . .

"Where's Phoenix?" Amy said, shoving the phone at

Dan because the flood of hot tears had obscured her vision. "Tell me you see Phoenix!"

"What are you talking about?" Dan asked.

"Phoenix," she said. "He's not in the photo, is he?"

Dan got up, grabbed the phone, and looked at the photo. His face whitened, and then two angry splotches of red appeared on his cheeks.

"It doesn't have to mean anything," he said. It was as if he couldn't bear to believe otherwise. "Maybe they just took him somewhere else."

"'And then there were six!'" Amy said bitterly. The plane was starting to blur as the shock coursed through her.

The Vesper phone chimed again. A text message appeared. The two siblings read it together.

```
Phoenix Wizard sat on a wall. Phoenix
Wizard had a great fall. All the Vespers'
horses and all the Vespers' men couldn't
put Phoenix together again. You didn't
really think that I would reward you for
your failure with the Jubilee? And as
you can see, the others paid a price,
too. I suggest you get to the United
States in the next 24 hours or another
Cahill will fall.

Vesper One
```

INFINITY RING

"We're members of a group called the Hystorians," the man said. "You wouldn't have heard of us, but our organization goes back many, many centuries. It was founded by the great philosopher Aristotle in 336 BCE. We've lasted in a continuous line ever since, united in a common goal to set right the world's course...before everything ends in the fiery Cataclysm that Aristotle himself predicted. Today you've given us the biggest breakthrough since he spoke of that vision. Time travel."

He paused and gave a long look to Sera, then Dak. **"History is broken, and we need your help to fix it."**

◪ SCHOLASTIC

SCHOLASTIC and associated logos are trademarks and/or registered trademarks of Scholastic Inc.   IRMAY12

Hi Buddies!

So sad about your friends.
What can I say . . . oops?
If you don't want another
"accident," head back to
the U.S. of A. as fast as your
kiddie feet will carry you.
I want the Voynich, and I
want it now.

No hard feelings!
Vesper One

CLIMBING THE LADDER
OF SUCCESS

After years of preparation, you finally have your diploma and you're ready to put all those hard-earned skills to use in your new career. You have big dreams of landing your dream job and starting your climb up the ladder of success. However, while you're dreaming remember that everyone has to start that climb on the bottom rung. While it may be frustrating to have to start out in an entry-level position, with the right attitude you can use that job to showcase your skills and your willingness to learn.

Jesus said that those who can be trusted with the little bit of responsibility they are given prove that they can be trusted with great responsibility. When you work hard at your new job, even when it isn't really the job you want, you prove that you will also work hard when you're given that promotion you really desire.

Jesus also said that those who want to be great must be servants to others. This can be applied to you in the workplace. Be willing to do the jobs that others don't want, and pitch in to help your coworkers even if it isn't in your job description. When you do, you'll show that you care about the success of others and aren't just concerned with your own interests.

When you strive to do your job in a way that pleases God, you'll find that you also please your employer. And when you do your best with enthusiasm, even when you're still on that bottom rung of the ladder, you'll find that it isn't long before you're asked to start climbing on up toward your dreams.

Worship

Ascribe to the LORD the glory of his name;
worship the LORD in holy splendor.

PSALM 29:2 NRSV

Oh come, let us worship and bow down;
Let us kneel before the LORD our Maker.
For He is our God.

PSALM 95:6-7 NKJV

The LORD loves justice
and will not leave those who worship him.
He will always protect them.

PSALM 37:28 NCV

He put a new song in my mouth,
a song of praise to our God.

PSALM 40:3 NCV

God is honored by all who worship him.

PSALM 149:9 NCV

WHAT IS WORSHIP?

What's the first thing that comes to your mind when you hear the word *worship*? Do you picture someone sitting in a pew at church with a hymnbook on a Sunday morning? Do you see old monks and nuns doing chants? Is that really all there is to worship?

Worship is so much more than singing songs in church. God created you uniquely, with your own special way of worshiping Him. Whenever you use the gifts and passions He has given you to show Him your love, you are worshiping Him.

When you give God the credit for helping you through all of your final exams and projects and getting you to graduation, that is an act of worship.

When you take a day off and spend it outside, breathing clean air and enjoying God's creation, that is an act of worship.

When you turn down a dream job across the country so that you can stay in your hometown and care for your ailing parent, this is an act of worship.

When you give up your precious free time to volunteer at a local homeless shelter, that is an act of worship.

When you laugh with joy as you play with a child, praising God in your heart for that little life, it is an act of worship.

When you cry with a friend who is dealing with loss— mourning with those who mourn—this, too, is an act of worship.

Worship is anything you do that shows your gratitude and love to God. Take the time each day to worship Him in your own special way. You bring joy to His heart whenever you use your own special gifts to praise Him.

TOPICAL INDEX